Josaphine's Lessons

BY G. A. HARVEY

Copyright © 2012 by G. A. HARVEY
First Edition – February 2012

ISBN
978-1-77097-109-7 (Hardcover)
978-1-77097-110-3 (Paperback)
978-1-77097-111-0 (eBook)

All rights reserved.

No part of this publication may be reproduced in any form, or by any means, electronic or mechanical, including photocopying, recording, or any information browsing, storage, or retrieval system, without permission in writing from the publisher.

Important: This is a work of fiction. Names, characters, places, and incidents are the product of G. A. Harvey's imagination, are used fictitiously, and are not to be construed as real. Any resemblance to actual events, locales, organizations, or persons, living or dead, is entirely coincidental.

Published by:

FriesenPress
Suite 300 – 852 Fort Street
Victoria, BC, Canada V8W 1H8

www.friesenpress.com

Distributed to the trade by The Ingram Book Company

TABLE OF CONTENTS

ACKNOWLEDGMENTS v

DEDICATION. vii

PREFACE ix

1) GERALD – THE FIRST OLDER MAN. 1

2) JUNIOR – MY FIRST TEENAGER. 5

3) DREW – THE DEVIOUS PLAYER. 9

4) PHIL – THE FIRST WHITE GUY 15

5) BONES – THE SKINNY MAN. 19

6) DENNIS – DON'T BLINK. 23

7) RICHARD – A SINLESS MAN. 27

8) BUBBA – HE'S NOT A REDNECK. 31

9) STEVEN – MY OWN GREEK GOD 35

10) ZACH – THE SMOOTH WHISPERER 39

11) DARRYL – O. M. G.. 43

12) TIMOTHY – THE AFTER-HOURS MAN. 49

13) BILL – 6'10" OF FANTASY 55

14) CHUCK – THE DAM MAN 61

15) BUTCH – WORK WITH IT. 67

16) ZEKE – THE SECOND WHITE GUY 71

17) TOM – THE THIRD WHITE GUY 75

18) DON – THE FOURTH WHITE GUY 79

19) WILL – JUST FRIENDS. 83

20) JACK – THE REPRIEVE. 89

21) CHARLES – WHEN NO IS NOT ENOUGH 93

22) JASON – MY FRIEND'S BROTHER 101

23) KENNY – I'M CLUELESS 105

24) ROGER – THE SHY ONE .109

25) JOE – THE PRIZE BULL 113

26) LARRY – THE MERCEDES OVERLOAD 117

27) MIKE – THE MONKEY MAN 121

28) LUCIUS – SALT AND PEPPER MAN 125

29) ELVIS – AN AFRICAN PRINCE 131

30) GEORGE – THE SECOND OLDER MAN 137

31) SAMUEL – THE THIRD OLDER MAN. 141

32) NAMELESS – THE POOL GUY. 147

33) ROBERT – NOT SATISFIED. 151

34) LEROY – THE STOP-OVER MAN 155

35) JAMES – THE TIRE MAN 159

36) MARK – SPECIAL LITTLE FRIEND. 165

37) LI – THE ASIAN MAN. 173

38) HENRY – THE DETECTIVE 181

39) ALEX – KISSING SHOULD BE OUTLAWED. . .187

40) STEPHAN – THE ISLAND PLEASER 193

About the Author 201

ACKNOWLEDGMENTS

I definitely want to thank my many friends, especially Sandra Bartley, Kim Boston, and Myra Sanders for the many nights of late conversations and laughter, for their support, encouragement, and patience. To my editor friends, Rochelle Ware and Tom Walker, thank you for patiently hanging tough with me over the years of the duration of this writing. To Joanne Ware, for copy editing at the last moment! Thank you!

To Lynn and Tim at FriesenPress, thank you for the confidence and for following up with me when I reached my many blocks. You are very special.

To the many readers, I hope you find laughter, understanding, enjoyment, and awe as you read the lessons learned—as I did while writing them.

Finally, to my daughter, for being so supportive and understanding; it hasn't been easy for us, but we made it through. You are truly my best friend.

DEDICATION

To my daughter Maurizia,

I'm so glad I learned to say your name,

It's music to my ears each time I hear it spoken

And, a reminder that there is a God with a sense of humor.

PREFACE

I invite you to sit down in my living room and have some sweet tea, or something stronger like a Long Island Iced Tea, my Absolute favorite. Join me as I recall a period of time in my life of sexual encounters. I am now an older, full-figured black woman living in the south, Georgia actually, and there is much in my life to remember from the ages of seventeen to thirty-five. Before my memory escapes me, let us see if we can get into some trouble!

This book, *Josaphine's Lessons*, is about the men and the sexy adventures I had with them. There are good and bad sexcapades, of course, plus some stories that are naughty enough that they probably should not be repeated at all. Some lessons were learned the hard way, so hopefully they will have a valuable impact on your life—or some will just plain make you smile! These sexcapades are not for the faint of heart or those who want to share their opinions. No way! It's for the person who can look at life's quirks and sexual situations and laugh, cry, or just say,"Damn!"—whichever you prefer.

Laughter is good for the soul. It's also delicious to sit around with friends and talk about sex with our sweet, stimulating refreshment. You will find some of them worth repeating to your friends, with life lessons learned at the end of each tryst. Still, the faint of heart, when it comes to sex, should proceed with caution while reading these chapters. However, the brave and curious will venture through each chapter, trying to figure out whom I am talking about, or if the sexcapade really was true or not. Naturally, the names have been changed to protect the not so innocent—and me, too. Happy Lesson Learning!

Important: This is a work of fiction. Names, characters, places, and incidents are the product of G. A. Harvey's imagination, are used fictitiously, and are not to be construed as real. Any resemblance to actual events, locales, organizations, or persons, living or dead, is entirely coincidental.

1

GERALD – THE FIRST OLDER MAN

Gerald: a smooth, sneaky, older man. He wooed me for a year before I finally surrendered to the gut-wrenching feelings beckoning my body to him. I was seventeen, and he was thirty-four when he winked at me from across the room in a community meeting. I couldn't believe a man so much older than me would be flirting with and interested in me.

After several months of community meetings he asked, "Can I give you a ride home?" Well, I just about wet my pants. I got in his 69' BMW and thought this was the coolest car I had ever been in. Gerald began taking me home after the meetings and leaving me with the most dangerous, all-consuming kisses. He was a fascinating, patient man who kissed like it was the last notes played in a symphony. My body rocked to his music and I secretly determined that I would follow to the finale. He brought me into a musical sweep that left me shuddering each time we kissed. I couldn't take leaving him before the last note would be played. Alas! The grand finale was yet to be played.

When I least expected it after a meeting one evening, Gerald said he was going to take me out to dinner. I didn't know what to say, but I heard myself mouth an "okay." Before he walked away, he stated that he wanted to end the night back at his apartment. My eyes flew wide open as he asked if I was up for such an evening. I felt nervous and self-conscious but responded with a definite nod. We had never gone out on a date together. I wanted him so badly but my emotions were running rampant the whole time. My mind and body were in a confused state of yes, no, yes, no. I was an emotional wreck because it would be my first time going all the way; but, I knew he could calm the fires he stoked in me when I was near him.

Dinner was at a fancy restaurant with glasses of white wine for me and a bottle of Port for him. I was a neophyte drinker, and after two glasses, I was feeling very lively and became brave enough to strike a teasing chord at that massive hunk of flesh across the table from me. I fluttered my eyes and whispered if he was planning on having me for dessert. Gerald smirked and said, "Of course, that's the plan." After feeling so cocky, I had the nerve to blush.

By the time we finished dinner, I was so full; I was so nervous that I ate all the food on my plate. I should have been carted from the restaurant in a piano crate, I thought. Gerald gently escorted me to the car and we headed for his place. As soon as we reached the front door I was ready to bolt for the bathroom. The nerves in my stomach were playing a heavy metal concert. Gerald must have thought I was nervous because of my upcoming participation in our sex performance, but that was taking second fiddle to the percolating food I consumed at the restaurant in my attempt to be suave and sophisticated.

After I took a soothing bath and went to the bedroom, Gerald was as naked as the day he entered the world. He strutted around in all his glory like it was an everyday occurrence. I had a towel wrapped around me, and he reached for me to plant one of his mind-disturbing kisses on my lips, my neck, and down my throat. I was already hot on the outside and inside—I was a blazing inferno! It was a wonder I didn't self-combust.

He took me by the hand and led me to the bed. He removed my towel and proceeded to conduct a different concert with his hands, along with the one my stomach played. He laid me down beside him and started to fan the fires consuming me while kissing me on my hips and below. He licked and kissed and found his way up my thigh and into the juncture of my sweet nectar. I rocked from the excitement, but also strained to fully capture the wonderment of this extraordinary melody he was playing. My stomach decided to resume its own concert—but how could I get up now and disturb the crescendo happening? I silently pleaded for my stomach to relax and behave while the grand finale was about to begin.

Gerald raised my legs around his shoulders and was ready to put his tongue in the honey pot, when my naughty stomach groaned and decided to introduce the wind section. It released a serious flat note. The sound was out of sync with the rest of the melody and pulsating rhythm being conducted over our bodies. The conductor looked at me with an amused expression and said, "I beg your pardon. Would you like to contribute to the concert in another fashion? I didn't think the winds were included in the program for the evening, were they?"

I rolled away and burst into a fit of laughter. "Smartass!"

Lesson learned– When being played like a well-strung orchestra, before participating, do not engage in gas producing foods that can introduce the wind section at the wrong time!

2

JUNIOR – MY FIRST TEENAGER

As my freshman year of college ran its course, my newfound hobby was starting to develop and younger guys were the target of choice. Having only had a large, bearded, rather soft muscled man for months, I was attracted by the hard muscles and thick thighs I saw in the gym. Junior caught my eye right away with his light skin and an afro the size of Jupiter. He was funny and he walked sort of penguin-like. All I could focus on was nineteen years of hard male flesh, flexing everywhere at once. I wanted just to touch him. The urge was so strong I couldn't resist, so I started dating him and kept my old friend on the side. My older gent had some other interests himself, so I busied myself with Junior.

Junior had an odd sense of humor, but he was kind and tall, and I loved playing with his hair. We were together for our first Christmas holiday and got invited to several holiday parties. He came by my house to pick me up for a party and spoke to my Mom in the den. As I gathered my things to leave, I noticed Mom was leaving too, going to her friend's dinner party. Light bulb, light bulb, I had a brilliant idea!

It was no work at all to get Junior on board with my idea, and after leaving the house we quickly went by the bootleggers for some cheap wine and doubled back to the house. We figured Mom would be gone for at least a couple of hours. We started toasting to our idea and began kissing in the den. We turned the TV on and then began taking off our clothes. We kissed half naked in the den on the floor, made a trail through the kitchen, and then to my room. I didn't have a soft carpet floor but I did have a very nice twin bed. We were hot and going at it like rabbits, intending to populate all of Connecticut when I saw the light come on in the kitchen and heard the water being turned on and off.

My heart about froze in my chest as I heard the refrigerator open and close and a glass taken out of the cabinet. I was tuned in to these sounds like long distance radar, because I didn't want to believe Mom was back home already! How could she be back so soon? Then, I thought, could we really have been playing around for such a long time? Either way, I was headed for big trouble.

For a minute, all I could think over and over was aw shit, aw shit, aw shit! Our clothes were thrown all around the kitchen and den. What to do, what to do, what to do? I tried to tell myself DON'T PANIC, but it wasn't working at all. Junior kept holding me and said, calm as could be, "Sounds like your Mom is back home."

"No shit, Sherlock!" Now, I often had a little cursing problem when I was really scared and this sure seemed the right time for it. I told Junior to be very quiet and let me think....Finally, I said whispering, "Let's pretend we are sleeping!" I knew it wasn't a good plan, but it was the only thing I could think of at this moment of temporary insanity.

We stayed in the room for another twenty minutes or so and stayed very, very quiet. I could hear my Mom in the den, and the TV getting louder and louder playing a Christmas Eve gospel show. In my mind, I could just see the baby Jesus all cozy in the manger and a heavenly choir singing, and thought I was going to Hell for sure. I felt caught, judged and punished already.

After thirty minutes, I figured Mom might have fallen asleep in her recliner like she did sometimes, and I might have a chance to go get our clothes. I threw some pajamas on and stalked through the kitchen picking up our discarded clothes. All safe so far, but then I looked around the doorway into the den, and just five feet away, next to Mom's chair, were Junior's pants and shoes. They may as well have been in Mom's lap, and there was no chance to get them secretly. How could things get worse? Easily, as I was finding out with each step I took. I felt like I was walking into thick-Mom trouble on purpose.

    I tiptoed in as quietly as I could and looked at Mom in the dim lighting. No escape! Time for my Oscar performance. I had to play it for all it was worth. I started walking in, playing all sleepy eyed and said, "Hey Mom, you're home. How was your party? I'm just getting Junior's clothes because he fell asleep in my room." I knew instantly my acting was not going to be an award winning debut. Mom immediately turned to stare and glared at me like she was catching me in the spotlight. She was so mad her eyebrows were crossed. Mom's stare would cut straight through bullshit without a sound, and this time I was catching the crossfire. I was sure her look would open the gates of Hell and make Satan tremble, and she was damn sure burning those eyes on me.

    She never said a word. I quickly got Junior's clothes together and headed back to my room. One surprise is never enough, I guess, because what did I see? Junior, standing in the middle of my room, naked as the day he was born, his erection flying at full mast. If I wasn't already going to burn in hell, surely now, I was going to be incinerated for all eternity.

    What an idiot! I threw his clothes at him and said, "Get dressed and meet me in the den. When you come through, speak nice to my Mom and then head straight for the front door! Do you hear me?" I might as well have been talking to a wall because his brain was not in charge. He had a shit-eating grin on his face and was pointing at his johnson, begging me to hop on. Granted, any other night I would have been on him like white on rice—but not now! Instead, I punched him in the gut. "GET DRESSED," I hissed. Didn't he realize the nightmare we were in? No, of course not. I knew he had a one-track mind right now, and I really couldn't blame him. Earlier, we had been too hot to handle and we had had no plans to stop. Mom's early return was a serious blow to the love making!

When he went through the den and headed for the front door to leave, he spoke to my Mom nice as could be and said, "Merry Christmas, Mrs. Sanders. Did you have a nice time at your party?"

Mom grunted something inaudible and stared at him with a killer glare, strong enough, that if looks could kill, he would've been beaten and stoned to death twice over. I kept shoving him towards the door. I was hoping this fiasco was almost over. The fool tried to kiss me good night right then and there, and I about took his head off with my fist getting him to go out the door.

When I turned around after closing the door, BAM! I had a three-layer carrot cake with cream cheese frosting smashed in my face and sliding down my pajamas to the floor. As I opened my mouth to speak, cake slid its way in, and I at least got to savor Mom's famous baking. That cake was so damn good, I licked it off my fingers; it about made up for the misery! But my Mom didn't speak to me for days. The silence was unbearable and really painful.

Lesson learned– When skipping out on a party and deceiving Mom, don't throw Junior's evidence around. You can't outsmart Mom! The results will be damning glares and a wasted carrot cake.

3

DREW – THE DEVIOUS PLAYER

Growing up in a large family, I was the youngest of eight. I had four older brothers and three older sisters. We all were about two or three years apart. We lived in a big, three-family house with cousins included, and there were always a lot of siblings and relatives with very tempting friends hanging around. Mom's simple rule was you had to have permission to date any friends of your brothers', sisters' and cousins'. Well, being the spoiled baby sister, I decided to put this rule to the test and see what would happen.

My youngest brother had several boys he ran around with, and they came to the house on a regular basis. Yearly growing up, we would all have snowball fights in our backyard or go swimming in the neighborhood. As I entered my teen years, I was filling out quite nicely and things were changing fast. My brother would often catch me kissing a boy in the hall, and he would act very protectively, telling them to get lost before he did something wicked or devious to them.

One day, he was furious because his friend Drew was at the house watching me wash dishes in my hot pants. They were the style back in the 70's, and "hot" meant too short and too tight. My brother nearly took Drew's head off and threatened to bury the both of us where we couldn't be found, if we so much as tried to see each other. He kicked Drew out of the house. I certainly wasn't getting his permission to date Drew; however, that didn't slow me down at all. I just dreamed of the day I could kiss that fine brother's juicy lips and play with his so very fine hair. He made my body vibrate like a tuning fork when he was staring at me. I was no different than any other teenage girl—I had a crush, even if it was my brother's friend.

Three years later with a lot of changes happening in our lives, Drew had taken to the streets as the player of the south side square. He fit the part and strutted himself around, taking drugs to a new level for him, but he never stopped being one fine specimen of a man in my eyes. He still caused my body to vibrate by just looking at me, and one day he stepped up to take his opportunity with me.

I was in college in my sophomore year and living in the dorms. I was seeing less of my older friend and hardly any of my teenage boyfriend, since he'd gone away to college in North Carolina. As I often did for fun, one night I drove home to my hometown from college and went club hopping. I loved to dance, and "grinding" (very slow, close dancing) was my favorite way to dance. That night in a club I ran into Drew. He smiled when he saw me, took me by the arm and led me outside to his car. We both looked around to see if my brother would appear. He drove a huge Lincoln Continental, money green, with doors that opened out from each other. Very cool car! He said to get in; he wanted to talk. All I could do was stand there and try to get my body not to go crazy. I was alone at last with Drew, and my brother was nowhere in sight. "There is a God," I thought and jumped into the front seat.

Drew had on a stylish, white wool coat and suit to match. I might have been desperately in need of being rescued from Drew, but my "saving" brother wasn't around at this moment, which was simply fine with me. I was ecstatic! As far as I was concerned, Drew was a wicked angel coming to rescue me just the way I needed and most definitely wanted. He slid close to me and without a word, grabbed my face in both of his hands and stuck his tongue in my mouth. As he stroked my jaw and head, he kissed me like he finally found water to quench

Josephine's Lessons

his thirst. I felt like I was drinking from a sweet well. This was heavenly, devilish, exotic kissing!

He was different than anyone else I had kissed. He tasted sexy, strong, and definitely sweet. I was virtually getting a contact high from the urgency of his kisses. We made out in that car for a while before he said, "I need to take care of some business and then I'll come back for you." I responded, "I need to get back to my college dorm room before curfew." He offered to drive me back when he returned. I knew where this was going, but how could I say no. I was with Drew at last and I wasn't quite sure of my senses. He made me feel so nice, naughty and wicked! A "yes" vibrated from my mouth and melted on his lips. He was too damn fine and irresistible for his own good and he knew it.

He put me out, and I floated back to the club for more dancing and drinking to wait for him. Two long hours later, Drew found me on the dance floor, and people just parted for him. Who was this man? I knew I should run before the halo turned into horns, but I just couldn't. I knew my curiosity and desire was going to get me one day, but dammit, tonight I was going back to my dorm room with him. I would just have to try to decide whether I was going to be in heaven or hell and find an escape route later.

We drove the forty-five minutes back to my dorm in record time. I held his hand all the way as he drove like a warrior in a chariot, goal in sight. I signed him in as a guest and we went to the top floor of the dorm. Women eyed him and even whistled at him. He oozed sexuality. I held my head high and silently pronounced that he was mine. He walked with all the confidence of a lion dominating his pack. I had to vibrate to a different pitch at this point. What was I going to do with this man? The one thing I knew for sure was what I could do *for* this man—right now!

Well, from that point on the rest of the evening moved like it was in slow motion, and every look and touch was electric and sizzling. Drew took a seat on the only place available, my bed. My roommate's side of the room was empty. She must be out for the night, I thought, which was fine by me. I watched Drew remove his coat and pimp hat, and then he handed them to me. Somewhere in the great beyond of thought, I said to myself, "Is that all you are going to take off?" I was beyond ready!

"I had no idea you were so anxious," he said and took off his jacket. The shirt he had on was silk and molded to him like a second skin. I started sweating just from the sight of his lean frame. He started to unbutton his pants and suddenly my arms were groaning from the weight of his clothing, and my eyes fastened themselves like glue to the front of his pants.

I gasped when he had no underwear on and his flesh jutted from under the tails of his shirt. "That's going to feel real good inside me," I said out loud, staring. He chuckled and said, "Why don't you find out?" Honey, I threw those clothes on my roommate's bed like they didn't exist anymore, and then hurled myself at him. We landed in a heap on my bed, and my head hit the wall so hard I saw stars. I hardly cared that I was so clumsy. He grabbed my body and slid on top of me while I was still fully dressed. But I felt his hands on my bottom raising me towards his hardness as he divested me of my pants and panties in one smooth tug. I heard him moan "Sweet Jesus," and I was so gone I could about see the clouds open and heavenly light shine around us as we slid together to begin that heavenly dance. He entered me and I screamed, but it was more from shock and surprise than a glorious feeling!

Things changed fast from glory to shock as I saw someone standing in the doorway, which was where the light had really come from! I instantly thought the Lord had sent my brother to chastise me and the devil was having a good laugh. I looked away from Drew's shocked expression to find my roommate standing in the doorway with half the girls' basketball team. We had a full house audience! Drew got up and pulled me in front of him to shield his nakedness, but the girls were already gawking at the size of him. I don't think they even saw his face.

Josaphine's Lessons

Damn! Next time I'll remember to slow down, lock the door, and put a sign out that reads "dreamy, angelic, and devilishly hot man in my bed. DO NOT DISTURB!"

Lesson learned– "Devious players" generally are bad for you. But once you feel your body humming and your senses tingling to make love, remember there is a huge valley between heaven and hell. Let the light shine and just don't forget to lock the damn door!

4

PHIL – THE FIRST WHITE GUY

Still in my sophomore year of college, I decided to broaden my horizons one night and went to a jazz club in New Britain with some friends. We were drinking screwdrivers and sipping wine when a short, Italian-looking white guy asked me to dance. At first, I reacted: "You talking to me?" But, he asked again and my girlfriend was literally pushing me saying, "Go on girl! Take that fine looking white man for a ride." I chuckled and said, "Why not!! We're supposed to be open-minded college kids, right?"

My girlfriend was leading by example. She was already dating a tall, good looking white guy who was living with her. Phil just happened to be shorter and fine. I'm 5'5" and looking back, he must have been about 5'7". But when he drew me into his embrace for the slow dance, I fit perfectly against his lithe anatomy. On the dance floor, it didn't take long to find out he was a great kisser too—my decisive weakness! How positively aggressive he was.

After a few dates, I decided to take him to my mother's for dinner. My Mom, who was at last talking to me again after my many previous adventures, fixed my favorite dinner for us. We were having Cornish hens with oyster stuffing, collard greens, mac and cheese and a 1,2,3,4, cake for dessert. (A 1,2,3,4 cake is a pound cake made with no liquids.) I was salivating all the way home. I asked Phil if he was nervous, but he was being brave and just puffed on his pipe and smiled at me.

We pulled up to the house and I could see my older brother and sister staring out the window. We climbed the stairs and opened the door into the living room. My brother and sister were on the couch snickering, and my Mom was standing in the archway to the dining room. She blurted, "What is this? I thought you were bringing a special guest for dinner!"

I tried to recover right away and said "Mom, this is my friend Phil." She seemed to get some control and manners, and politely shook his hand and asked him to have a seat, but she glared at me with that killing Mommy eye, and I knew to follow her out of the room. She went in her bedroom and closed the door behind us. Aw hell, I thought, I'm in real trouble again. Mom continued to glare at me and asked if I was dating this young man. I answered with a defiant, "Yes!" Brave or not, this was without a doubt the wrong answer! This time, Mom was so angry her freckles were dancing across her face and she started telling me how wrong it was. I could smell the food coming from the kitchen and I was momentarily distracted from the tirade my mom was spewing. It was hard to concentrate! I focused back to what she was saying when I heard, "You can date them, work with them, sleep with them, but you don't mix the blood." I was totally lost. "Mom, what are you talking about? I haven't slept with Phil. He's just a friend." Her expression told me clearly that she was not convinced but didn't push any further. She left the room and went to the kitchen to bring dinner to the table.

All evening, even with all my favorite foods on the plate before me, I tasted nothing! Those words "don't mix the blood" were floating around my head. Small talk circled the table between my brother, sister and Phil. I couldn't think of a thing to say the whole time. Mom just continued to wordlessly glare, and her words kept ringing in my ears. In the end, I didn't even want to stay for dessert. I remember thinking to myself, "I must be crazy. That cake was made for me." I had intended to eat at least three pieces and tonight should have

Josaphine's Lessons

been nice and special. But Phil wanted to go and I couldn't blame him. To top it all off, my brother was being a real asshole, too. I'd safely say the evening did not go well, yet I wasn't going to let it change my plans so easily.

We left after I wrapped up some dinner and cake for later and headed for Phil's place first, which was on the way to my college. He didn't have his own place but rented a room in the basement of his sister's house. We went in through the kitchen only to find that his sister also had food on the table for us. I was surprisingly hungry and ate the most amazing spaghetti and meatball dinner, this time under the different glare of his sister. It wasn't as bad as my house, at least! We talked some to make polite conversation and then retired to Phil's room.

I sensed this was the night for sex and I was facing a rather big decision at this point. Desire versus sanity! I had never seen a white man naked before and my curiosity was raging forward again. Phil asked me to dance to some jazz music he put on and I glided to his arms for that perfect fit. Okay, I could do this. He began kissing my neck and massaging my back. His hands were everywhere all at once. I was guided towards his bed as our hips swayed together for that dance known for all time.

He took my clothes off first and then his. He stared at me like I was a bowl of milk chocolate ice cream he was going to devour. I asked him to turn off the lights, but he refused and then I looked down at him. "Aw shit, I thought. What did I go and do that for?" His member was wiggling at me and was white, red and purple. It looked like an alien was pushing through the dark hair of his front region. I looked again and it kept wiggling and then winked at me. I remember clearly being stunned; frozen; my desire just lost in a moment. He came towards me and I simply froze up...oh, what to do, what to do! I squeaked out some question I don't remember at all, and he gently pushed me down on the bed for his answer. I felt his alien trying to phone home and closed my eyes yearning the darkness. I just gave in to whatever was going to happen. Phil entered me and he pushed left, then he pushed right...and soon it was over. The alien went limp in my womanhood and it was time to get the hell out of dodge.

Lesson learned– Don't mix the blood like Mom said, because it could resemble something white, red and purple and be a cousin to an alien.

5

BONES – THE SKINNY MAN

I traveled quite a lot in college because I was involved with various student organizations. One organization, for instance, had me traveling to a black student union dance in Storrs, home to the famous University of Connecticut, UConn.

There were plenty folks at this dance and it was hot, sweaty, smelly and funky. Just my kind of party! The tall, quite thin president of the black student union asked me to dance a slow jam, and I thought immediately that this is going to end badly. My instinctive radar was in full swing, but I didn't listen to the warnings very well, I'm afraid.

Slow dancing is an art form, and you either have it or you don't. You can two step it, round house, or just hold on for dear life and let the man grind you into oblivion. The latter must be done in the darkest corner possible, of course, since it's quite naughty, but oh, so delightful. It was clear though that President "Bones" was not the kind of guy to slow dance. He especially was not someone to grind with because he was just too damn skinny. I was a soft, full, curvy girl and the contrast would cause bruising.

As the black student president from my college, however, I was obligated to be nice, and I accepted his hand. It was sweaty and very pencil like. He put his arms around my waist, and I automatically placed mine around his neck. His neck was very thin and I could even feel his veins. He felt like a wet piece of straw.

I didn't think I was going to make it, but thankfully there was a ray of hope. The song playing was one of my favorites, "For the Love of You," by The Isley Brothers. Great love song for bumping and grinding for eight minutes with lots of moans and groans. I would get by with singing along. I would get lost in the song and pretend Bones weighed a lot more. He was tall, though, and I had him by several pounds of girl flesh, making for a decidedly poor match. His whole body seemed to fit between my cleavage.

Now, how we got from the gym where we were dancing (more than one dance because he was surprisingly good at it), to his dorm room still remains a mystery to me. We were in darkness with only some light from the moon casting slivers of soft shadows around the room. How appropriate for Bones and me that night. We got naked somehow, which also remains another mystery. I don't remember any of the intermediate steps along the way—it just somehow happened.

I do remember that he was talking to me about how good this was going to feel, when he reached to pull me into him and quickly elbowed me in the eye. He started a suave move to the right and another elbow jammed me in the stomach. Next thing I knew, I was entangled with a mass of very pointy bones. I thought he felt like the Grim Reaper. I simply couldn't handle it anymore!

All of a sudden and in a rush, the door opened and his roommate barged in. I screamed and the roommate started asking questions about what was going on. Poor Bones was on the floor gasping for air, because one of my meaty thighs had just smashed the living daylights out of his narrow balls. It seemed my intuition at the start had been right. This was the unfortunate ending for Bone's intended pleasure for the night! I simply sashayed my buxom self across the room for my clothes and asked where the ladies room was. I'm sure his roommate got his questions answered when he aided Bones off the floor.

Josaphine's Lessons

Lesson learned– Making love to skinny guys can be hazardous to various body parts and ruinous to your night life. It required far too much safety coordination for this full-figured woman's dance party! It pays to listen to your gut instincts!

6

DENNIS – DON'T BLINK

One summer night I was sitting in a bar with a girlfriend. While I was looking out the window, a fine specimen of a black man blocked my view. I felt that all too familiar tremble and asked my girlfriend sitting next to me, "Who's that delicious looking piece of chocolate cake?" She didn't know, but as we were watching the spectacular view, he turned around and headed into the bar. We were caught staring, so I decided to take full advantage of the situation.

I boldly said, "Hey you, my girlfriend was admiring your body and how wonderful you look, especially in those leather clogs." My girlfriend slapped me so hard across the back I fell off the bar stool right into his arms. He instinctively caught me and oh, he was strong and smelled so good. I was a goner in the blink of an eye.

I asked, "What's your name?" He just grinned, and set me back on the bar stool and went to talk to some other guys at the end of the bar. I watched his every move, especially his feet. Those clogs were so nice and the way his butt looked in those pants, I was dying. I couldn't tell you what his eye color was, but I knew from staring at those pants hugging that tight butt that he was not wearing drawers tonight.

By this point in my investigational love career, I thought my radar was well developed and never wrong. When he went back outside I followed, leaving my girlfriend to nurse both our drinks.

"Excuse me, sir, but I didn't catch your name back there!"

"My name is Dennis and I'm not your sir!" he shot back.

Without missing a beat I came back with, "Well, can you be something else then?" I thought, oh man, maybe I'm taking this aggressive pursuit to a new level! He smiled really big and I could see two rows of pearly whites and a little five o'clock shadow. Damn, he was fine and just too damn sexy for underwear to be on that appendage, let alone clothes. He strutted towards his car, a sweet Lincoln Continental (my favorite car), and asked if I needed a ride. Did he already know my reputation for getting in cars with guys I'm attracted too? How could he?

My friend came out of the club just as I gravitated to his car and *rescued me* with, "It's time for our card game, and we need to leave now so we won't be late." Damn, Damn, Damn. "Okay, be right there!" When I turned back around he had already driven off, leaving a misfortune for me.

A few days later, I was walking past a shoe store in the mall and saw the familiar sight of a butt in tight pants and a pair of clogs. I ran into that store almost on autopilot and sat down.

"Hello, its Dennis right?"

"Yes, do I know you?"

"I was the girl from the bar the other night that you offered a ride to and drove off."

After some idle chit chat he asked me to meet him back at the bar when he got off work. I agreed heartily and left the store. I wasn't going to play cards tonight and nothing was going to interfere this time.

Later that night we met at the bar, and he asked to take me for a ride. I wasn't in school then, and I couldn't take him to a dorm room, so we drove around talking, which was quite pleasant and went on for hours. Of course, gas was much cheaper back then. You could drive to the moon and back on a tank of gas, it seemed. In the end, it should be no surprise that he ended up sneaking me into his room.

He was staying with his grandparents in a room in the attic, so we had to be quiet and move real fast, which felt appetizingly naughty. We didn't do much talking once the kissing started. I never knew a guy's buns could feel so tight and luscious. His butt was so fine I just wanted to bite it. He placed me on his bed and I watched him undress. I had been sure he didn't wear underclothes and I was right—not a stitch. He put his clothes on a chair along with mine and joined me on the bed. I was so nervous. Me, the aggressive one! He looked gorgeous all over and very muscular. We kissed and rolled around on the bed and then he knelt before me and placed his hardness at my entrance.

I closed my eyes and waited for the heavenly feeling that comes at this point in my mental script. I was pumped and ready to see stars. He brought me up to him and entered me and then pushed. One stroke, two strokes and his buns got real tight in my hands and amazingly, he was finished. I looked at him and started to say something but he was already rising and putting his clothes back on. I thought this couldn't be happening. Could my fabulous "love attraction" be broken? Surely, my wonderfully tight-ass friend would do more? What signs did I miss that I should have seen? But alas, he threw my clothes at me and said, "Let's get ready to take you back to the bar."

Lesson learned– Just because the outside packaging looks delicious and delectable, it doesn't mean the inside is going to satisfy your hungry, overactive sex drive. Try not to look too surprised when there is nothing you can do. It's very disappointing to realize the tight-ass man is a *wham bam, thank you ma'am!*

7

RICHARD – A SINLESS MAN

Sometimes looking at a very dark man can scare you. I was staring at this guy, Richard, who was blacker than midnight, but he had the best skin and features I had ever seen. He looked carved from black marble. His teeth were white and his lips were full and tasty looking, and I started that all too familiar tremble. I wanted to touch him all over and see if his skin was that color in areas not seen by the naked eye. Richard approached me at the bar and smiled. Hmmmm!! I felt sure this would be an interesting night. He was so striking in his looks that I was immediately entranced. I had unstoppable wicked thoughts as my eyes glued onto him and decided to make my approach fast and straight forward.

"You want to go home with me?" He laughed and said, "Aren't you Eddie Sanders' baby sister?" Damn, I had hoped he wouldn't remember I was the youngest sister. I smiled in return and said, "The offer still stands."

I could see the wheels turning behind his eyes. What he wouldn't give to be able to bed a Sanders sister and get away with it, without the ass kicking of his life from my unforgiving, older brothers. I didn't have to worry however; the hook was already in motion.

We drove back to my place, which was in a nearby town, because I was sharing an apartment with a girlfriend who was also in summer sessions. She was gone for the weekend and I had the place to myself. This was coming together perfectly.

I asked Richard if he wanted a drink, and he followed me to the kitchen for a beer. I handed him the beer and went in for a kiss without a moment of delay. I wanted his lips to be as juicy as they looked. He jumped back and wanted to know if anyone else was in the apartment. He looked scared now that the reality of spending the night with me might be coming to fruition.

I grabbed the front of his shirt and pulled lightly. He didn't budge; rock solid. I was determined to move this ebony marble in more ways than one. I went in for the kiss again, and the second try worked as I was at once crushed—WHAM—against all that hardness from chest to knees, with a nice large bulge in the middle. I rocked against it and moaned as the kiss deepened and we started walking backwards to the bedroom. Richard, I was quite sure, was becoming erect to my plan.

Our clothes were coming off faster than the Venus Williams serve, and soon I was naked and he had on only some boxer shorts. Oddly old looking boxers too. So, okay, I thought maybe he was into preserving his gonads. Whatever…but when I reached to stroke him, he slapped my hand away.

I groaned from the sting and said, "What's the matter?" He responded that a woman isn't supposed to touch a man's "ding a ling." I couldn't believe it! I had to pause for a moment. This man had me by at least twelve years and he was calling his johnson a "ding a ling." Once more my intuition must be malfunctioning somehow. I should have sent his "ding a ling" ass out the door, but no, not me! I was too hooked and horny to let him go now.

I asked if anyone had ever touched him all over before and he said, "Never!"

"Okay, so how about a massage?" I said, swerving us onto another path. Perhaps that would divert him from being so sensitive.

"Only on my back!" he said.

Josaphine's Lessons

"Sure, lay down on the bed and I'll rub you down with some oil." His back looked like it was carved from the ancients and it rippled under my touch. Oh, those muscles were nice and hard and he was tight, very black and shiny. He had the look of a sculptured statue, just right for looking, smoothing, touching. My mind was fantasizing on how good this body was going to feel crushed against me from head to toe, doing that old-fashion dance. Perhaps we'd get this right after all. I thought it would be fine if I simply took everything a step at a time and at the right speed. I didn't want to scare him off.

I just had to look at his ass too, and this should be the time for the next move, I thought. I started to reach in his boxers and smooth my hand over his tight bottom, when—WHAM! He quickly moved again and his hand was on my wrist tugging me over to the side. In a moment he was on top of me. Hmmmmm! Maybe he's a tad sensitive to my touching him.

Surprised, I asked, "Are you okay?" He looked at me and started to kiss me. Again, that thought of maybe you should send his ass packing was at the front of my brain instead of hiding in the rear, when all of a sudden his boxers were gone and he thrust his hardness inside me with no fanfare at all. In the place of thinking it through and trying to set a romantic setting, we were doing it finally—so I let it go again!

I wasn't hurt, but I was certainly shocked that this fine looking black specimen of a man was lacking in the foreplay department. Perhaps he took the idea of "old-fashioned" to a new level for his generation, but I damn sure was not finished when he said, "ugh, ugh, push, push," and the dance was over; quite done. The beautiful sculpted statute turned into a molded soft lump of clay.

"Ah, that was the best ever!" he said as he rolled off me to the side. He was asleep in ten seconds flat, and I was left staring at the ceiling, thoroughly awake and unsatisfied.

Okay I thought, so what's a highly motivated, still horny, hot, sexy woman supposed to do? Here I am lying next to this giant of black marble and he is asleep. I hadn't gotten a chance to stir up the possibility of an orgasm let alone have one, so I very naturally decided to make one appear by myself.

I was in the throes of reaching that trembling, shaking and eye-crossing orgasm when I felt Richard pushing me. He literally said, "What the frick and frack are you doing?"

Interrupted—and—rudely I said, "What does it look like?"

He put on his boxers even while he was still lying next to me and started pointing his finger at me, shouting, "You are going straight to Hell for the sin you just committed! Jesus is watching you and you are never supposed to touch your tutu like that either." He jumped up from the bed and grabbed his shirt to put on. I couldn't have stopped the words escaping my lips if I wanted too. "Are you kidding me? How old are you Richard? I don't have a "tutu" mister, I have a pussy!"

He gasped and shouted, "Never mind that and don't use that nasty word. I'm not going to Hell with you and I'm leaving before Jesus strikes you down right here!" I was simply too shocked to move. He dressed faster than another Williams' high speed serve and headed out the door, all the while shaking his head and condemning my actions. The word *hypocrite* came quickly to mind! And to top it all off, his parting words to me were, "You are one nasty Smith sister and I am going to tell your brother!"

Lessoned learned – When your brothers' friends are off limits to you, it might be for a very good reason! Try to at least find out how religious a man might be before you engage in sinful activities. Some other things are best done in private still.

8

BUBBA – HE'S NOT A REDNECK

Bubba was a beautiful Portuguese man with rich, black wavy hair that just made you want to run your hands through it. I had known him for years and never came close to a sexual encounter with him. I'd often thought of what it would be like to sleep with him, but the right time never presented itself.

It seemed we were destined to be just friends without benefits. When I met him at the bar, I didn't hesitate to buy him a drink, having thoughts of a fling always in the back of my mind.

After several drinks and some great conversation, I told Bubba that I had to juggle my time that night. I had to make it back to my apartment for a hair appointment in the late evening. I'd met a promising hairdresser who moonlighted on the side from her shop, and I had lined her up for that night. By that point, we both knew we were headed for some playtime and it was just a matter of planning.

After telling Bubba about my schedule, he offered to take me back home, hang out while I got my hair done, then spend the night and bring me back to the club tomorrow to pick up my car. It sounded like a great plan and neither of us had other plans to arrange, so off we went to my apartment for my appointment. I thought I was finally getting that fine Portuguese man in the sack at last, after so many years!

When we arrived at my apartment the hairdresser was already waiting for me. I jumped out of the car quickly, made my apologies, and introduced her to Bubba. I could tell Bubba was a little taken back when he got an eyeful of the hairdresser. She was easily six feet tall with long shapely legs to match, sheathed in fishnet stockings and an afro the size of a small moon, creamy light-skinned and extremely beautiful. Knowing this hairdresser, I hadn't thought I would have competition, but I'd guessed wrong!

I laughed as I picked Bubba's chin off the ground and hurried us all upstairs to my apartment. I changed my clothes and set up in the kitchen while Bubba and the hairdresser chatted and got to know one another.

A pang of jealousy came over me for Bubba not lusting after me like that, but from the way Bubba's eyes glued themselves the hairdresser, I already knew my evening plans were changing. One more time, I just figured it was my destiny to be Bubba's friend without sex benefits.

The hair dresser made quick work of my haircut, and it was as great as her previous work. I was excited about it and got ready to go out to a nightclub to show off my stuff! As much as I wanted to score with that fine Portuguese man, I had consciously changed from focusing on sex-now-with-Bubba, to thinking it will happen one day, but maybe not right now.

I wasn't surprised in the least when Bubba asked if he and my new hairdresser could stay in my apartment for a while and "chill out." I fought back the jealousy that overtook me like a tidal wave and settled for telling him, half playfully and half seriously, that he better not be "messin" with my hairdresser. He might not realize what he was in for and definitely getting into!

He just smiled and assured me that it would be an evening of getting to know her and nothing else, but he would leave if I was uncomfortable with the situation. Oh, he was suave, but it was damn straight I was uncomfortable. It was very clear I wasn't getting Bubba in the sack and that I was losing out to those reach-all-the-way-to-the-heavens legs, but I held back my reactions. Disappointed as I was, I stayed calm, cool, and collected about it, and let them chill out. Bubba was obviously intent on what he wanted, like a master of the game.

I remember thinking over and over that one day, someday, Bubba and I would hook up and chill out, too. Bubba was a sweet friend for many years and I had plenty of time to make another move. My mind was cleared and focused, so I left them to discover each other. I went out to meet my friends in the club without a care that I would have to wait to make my next move on him.

Even so, after just a half hour of clubbing I wanted to—*had to*—go back and spy on Bubba and the hairdresser. I couldn't stand it—I had to be nosy and the urge was simply too strong. I asked a friend to drive me to my apartment and he readily agreed. He thought he was getting in the sack tonight.

We stopped and bought a bottle of wine with an excuse already made up that the club wasn't working for us, and we were going to watch a movie. Since my friend was quite nice looking, I thought maybe I could make Bubba a little jealous in return. I remembered it seemed fair to me at the time to do this, and the choice Bubba made was clearly physical in his mind. The hairdresser was definitely a sexy looking thing.

Well, I didn't have to worry about that situation after all. We arrived at the apartment and when I approached the door, I saw a hastily written note attached. It read:

Bubba is passed out on the kitchen floor, but it is not my fault. He fainted while we were kissing. His hands started massaging the right spots for me, but felt too similar to him. You know the reason...
See you at your next appointment!

Lesson learned- You don't have to tell all you know about your hairdressers. Friends who stray from you might get a handful more than they bargained for. Because truly, "Only the hairdresser knows for sure!"

9

STEVEN – MY OWN GREEK GOD

During my college days, I sometimes drove a sleek, gold '63 Cadillac that belonged to my roommate, the kind with the batman tailfins and all. We would cruise around town in that thing like queens. I was in the driver's seat one summer day and I swung us by a busy basketball park, which to my mind seemed a natural hunting ground for some steamy, hot, muscular men without shirts and in shorts.

It was crowded with pumped-up guys competing for the score and bragging rights on the courts. It was a hotbed of action, and even professional players would come by this park sometimes for the joy of ruling these well-known courts with bragging rights. Of course, with a park full of jostling men, there were lots of women cruising, too, and we weren't alone.

I slowed when we spotted a group of men standing on a nearby corner, and we approached to get a better look. I found myself staring straight at a pair of the tightest jeans on a brother I'd ever seen.

He honestly made me think of a Greek god, and I nearly forgot I was driving in traffic. His front was so bulged that I just reacted and pulled over as though I was on complete autopilot. My mouth had a mind of its own, too, and as we pulled to a stop I shouted, "Hey, you, come here!"

That un-lady like, come-on line naturally works fine from the front seat of a fashionable car, plus I have to say, I looked pretty fine myself. I had his attention, no problem.

This bulging Greek god sauntered over to the car and looked in. My roommate was the shy one and just grinned from the passenger seat, but I continued to boldly stare, and without a moment's delay I blurted out, "Lord Jesus there is a God!" There was no subtlety required here. Traffic was going to have to wait while I looked at this God-given specimen of a man.

I asked the stranger his name, and he said Steven. I asked for his phone number, and he received mine as well. Traffic was backing up and folks were getting really impatient for us to move along, but the job was accomplished. I continued on around the park and headed to our apartment.

The next day I called my bulging god, and his voice seemed as sensual and attractive on the phone as his looks had been in person. We talked for hours, and I found we had no mutual friends. Yeah, perfect! That was a good thing, as I didn't want to share my Greek find with anyone else and wanted no more entangled friendships.

He was a grown city man and I was a college girl, which might not be a really good mix, but my mind was on the statuesque man's huge bulge in that second skin of tight jeans.

We arranged to meet the next day at my apartment while my roommate went home for the weekend. Normally, I would accompany her, but putting that off was a decision I made easily. When Steven arrived, he didn't disappointment me either, as he had on the tightest jeans I have ever seen on a man again. He knew how to advertise himself, and I looked him over from head to toe to ass. He was gorgeous all over, every inch. I was hooked, hooked, hooked.

Then he smiled, and my fantasy came to a stop like a steel train hitting a brick wall. He was missing some front teeth, both top and bottom. Just gone—not even there; the places for those important, make-a-first-impression front teeth, left completely blank. I'd been so completely distracted I'd never really looked in his face when I pulled over! My eyes never traveled above his neck until right then. I had to do some quick thinking. "Damn," I thought, "Maybe if I don't talk to him he won't have to open his mouth." I sounded selfish as could be, and in view of those super tight pants, I just couldn't make myself care.

He came in and I made it past this first hurdle, somehow, and we settled down to talk for a while and had something light to eat. But then he started to kiss me. What was I going to do? The situation was becoming critical again, fast. I'd never kissed anybody with missing teeth before, and I had no idea how to "maneuver" the encounter. I went with the moment and had to make it work.

I was thinking that if I close my eyes, I could pretend he has all thirty-twos, and we'll see what happens. He came in for a tongue-filled big kiss, and I felt his hard chest against me. I forgot all about his mouth and my mind traveled south, focusing on that delicious looking bulge in his jeans. He took my hand and placed it on his erection, and my worries about what to do vanished completely with my doubting thoughts.

I was in heaven already and he was hard as a rock. Everything else disappeared from my brain. The texture of his jeans and me stroking his length alone was just about enough to burst my bubble. I couldn't wait another second and jumped up to lead him to my room. I remember thinking that we can always fix his teeth, and then everything would be perfect. The teeth could wait, but that sausage in his pants won't wait another second!

I sat on the bed to undress and asked him to take off his clothes for me. He laughed and unbuttoned his shirt. I looked at that smooth hairless chest and held back a very large gasp. I wasn't new at this, but he looked like a marble god times ten, and that chest gave new meaning to "six-pack abs." He began to unbutton his jeans. Now we'll get to see how he gets out of those painted-on things!

He began to tug them down and before I could blink, he pounced on me naked and ready to immediately thrust something that resembled a very large, blunt object into me. That swinging monster was immediately daunting more than I could handle, and I slowed things down as I scooted back and sat up. I didn't have on my glasses, but I didn't need them, as there was no denying the appendage coming at me resembled a third arm. More description and a measuring tape answer won't help. It was simply huge, huger, humongous, I tell ya!!!

I held up my hands and looked at him sputtering, "That thing's not going to fit in me!" He laughed again and responded with, "Let's just try and see!" I was scared shitless, but how was I going to get out of this one? I cursed myself for being greedy. If I had known, I would have left this Greek god-man on the corner and kept on going. I thought, "This is not only going to hurt, it's going to rip me in two!"

Much to my delight and reassurance, he was very interested in foreplay and took a lot of time for me to adjust. When the moment arrived for him to enter me, he was able to put it in without as much trouble as I'd feared. There was no doubt of its immense size, and I felt this "third arm" reaching inside me like it was trying to come up and tickle my throat. I felt like if I coughed, his johnson was going to come out my mouth and wink at me. He was up inside me as far as I wanted him to go, pushing my insides around with every move. By that point, it was no longer a question of ecstasy and joy as much as one of simple survival. I wouldn't be surprise if my uterus came out with him.

Pain and glory seemed completely mixed together, but the alarm never left and the pain was in the lead! I honestly thought I was about to get busted open and screw up any prospect of having kids, so I did what any respectable, upset woman would do in a time of excruciating pain and crisis: I took it as long as I could, then I grunted big and hard two times, faked an orgasm, and "fainted" from the exertion!

Lesson learned– Know your limits, because when the bulge you are looking at is bigger than one you've ever seen, it might also be bigger than your womanhood can handle! You can always grunt twice, fake an orgasm, and dramatically faint.

10

ZACH – THE SMOOTH WHISPERER

Zach was a teenage love of my life. When he was sixteen and I was fourteen, we kissed a great deal. From that promising start, I soon lost all that sweetness when he went into the service. He was the smoothest boy, and then man, I ever knew. I don't mean his complexion—I mean his ways of walking, talking, jiving and conniving. When he spoke, it was a *smooth whisper!*

Of course, he'd passed my first big test, being a great kisser. He could melt me in minutes, and his kissing made me weak in the knees, thighs and arms, just everywhere. One day years later, we met in a bar completely by chance. I was happily shocked to see him and he was, too. We greeted each other enthusiastically and started talking of old times, and how we used to make out whenever or wherever we could without getting caught.

We ordered drinks that I ended up paying for somehow, and then we decided to go for a walk. My Mom's house was down the street from the bar, and he offered to walk me home since I was staying there for the time being. I didn't know what to expect from Zach, but he seemed genuinely glad to see me, and I was game for whatever might happen.

Mr. Smoothness whispered in my ear as we continued walking that he wasn't simply happy to see me, he wanted to taste more of me. I had to smile to myself. I was a little tipsy, but I was not so far gone that I'd get conned by his silky words. But there was no denying the lure of those past passions. We'd only ever kissed before, and the thought of going further was definitely enticing.

We reached the hallway to my house and started kissing at the bottom of the stairs. I really wanted to sneak him up those stairs and into my room, but I didn't need a repeat of getting caught in the house and more of Mom's powerful staring. We got pretty hot right there in the hall, and I couldn't slow down. His hands were everywhere as he started to lift my skirts and pull my panties down. I froze. He meant for us to get it on in my hallway! The risk and heat of it all made me all kinds of dizzy. Oh Yeah! We were going to get it on.

He wasted no time and pulled his erection out and flipped me around to enter me from behind. I was so nervous and dry, dry, dry, but I wasn't thinking straight, either. Now, anybody else might have backed off and slowed down, ready to move the location— but not Zach.

He leaned over my back, continued to caress me and whispered into my ear something dirty and then something a little dirtier, and then dirtiest still, and in moments I felt the rush of juices flowing down my body. He flipped me around facing him and dropped to his knees to kiss me in that most intimate, delightful and moistening way. Instead of dry, dry, dry, I was now wet, wet, wet!

I remember it was so intense, I could hardly stand up. He didn't have long enough hair for me to grab his head, so I slithered my hips down on his face and reached back to grab the banisters behind me. We were making so much noise that I feared getting caught at any moment. I just knew Mom was going to come down the stairs; or, one of my brothers, sisters, or cousins would open a door to see what the hell was going on.

It's amazing what the mind can process when one is having intense, oral sex performed on them. At that moment really, nothing else mattered but that wonderful feeling. I wanted more! He finished feasting on me to readiness and stood up, turning me around to urgently slide into me from behind. I lurched forward and banged my head on the stairs—but felt no pain. All I could feel was the thrill of this man so deep inside me.

He pumped and pumped and pumped, and I took every bit of it until we both reached a climax that seemed to shatter the walls. Thoughts of the danger and risk had completely vanished, and I remembered feeling like we nearly burned the house down. I know I was grinning from head to toes as we recovered. We had finally gone beyond kissing after all this time, and I was truly satisfied, right there at the bottom of the hallway in my Mom's house.

He turned me around and kissed me on the cheek as we finished getting ourselves straight. When he was ready to leave, he asked to go to the movies with me the next day, and I nodded my head silently and happily. I was still unable to bring a coherent thought into my mind, and I hardly could register it when he asked me to loan him twenty dollars for the tickets. I felt weak with satisfaction and on top of the world, with no thought of Mr. Smoothness or my earlier determination. All I could do was wonder how to climb up the stairs to bed in my dazed state.

I reached into my purse and handed him a twenty easy as pie. I'm sure I was thinking about how I was going to get some more of this wonderful heat the next day! He kissed me and left me there in the hallway, and I literally had to sit down on the stairs for a moment until I could make my knees carry me up three flights of stairs.

I sniffed, and then I sniffed again as my nose got my attention on its own initiative. Oh, God! Trouble—more trouble! That little, enclosed hallway was saturated with the smell of somebody getting their freak on—in a big way. My thoughts turned to escaping, and I quickly ran up the stairs, straight to my room. I clearly recall having fabulously naughty thoughts and dreams the whole night without a care in the world....

I waited the next day for Zach to pick me up for the movies, but he never showed, and my glowing happiness started to fade fast. I finally found a friend and went out to the clubs around ten o'clock that night. Along the way, we saw Zach standing in front of a house I knew was connected to drugs. He didn't see me, but the friend with me knew him. She commented that it was rumored Zach was back and on the strip. Damn! The sex had been awesome, but that did it for me. When I heard that rumor and saw where he was hanging out, I suddenly felt sick inside, knowing I'd been pimped for twenty dollars of sex in a hallway.

Lesson learned– Never, ever handle money and sex at the same time. Your head can't think straight, and it can easily lead to upset and disappointment, no matter how good the sex. Because in the end, I was pimp'd, pump'd and punk'd!

11

DARRYL – O. M. G.

On one of my many college trips, I visited Washington, D. C., for the first time as our representative for homecoming entertainment. I was there for four full days listening to bands audition to play at our school. Our school was not very popular, but we were invited to view the bands, none the less.

I was sitting in the back of the auditorium daydreaming how we could get together the kind of money to get a hot band like Chaka Khan, or Earth, Wind and Fire, when someone approached and interrupted my thoughts by asking the time. Looking at my watch, I realized it was late in the evening and remembered I was looking forward to going out dancing with friends. But when I looked up and saw the rather imposing figure asking the time, my mind went completely blank. He was over six feet tall and was wearing a stunning, full-length, rabbit fur coat. Wrapping my head around the big impression standing there, I managed to tell him the time, and he asked me if I was with a band. I told him I represented a school and was waiting to go out on the town. He asked me if I had ever been to D.C. before, and I said, "No."

He was wearing a stylish hat at a rakish angle that covered a lot of his face, so I didn't see his eyes, but I could hear mischief in his smooth, baritone voice. He asked me out on a date for the evening and smoothly promised to have me back before the sun came up. Good looking, but brash! So I refused. He was by no means done, and asked if I wanted to go to a club. Well played, I thought. I was planning on it anyway, so it might be possible, and I screened him a bit more by asking which club. If he named a hundred D.C. clubs, I wouldn't have known the difference. Then he said the magic words: "Henry's in Georgetown," where I'd heard Roberta Flack was playing.

Lightning striking would not have amazed me more—I couldn't believe my luck! Like a light switch, my inner mischief maker came on and took charge of my mouth. I agreed on one condition, that he had to have me back to the conference center before sunrise. He laughed a rich laugh and I knew I was in for a good time. He was definitely not to be taken lightly.

When we reached the club, Roberta Flack had already performed, and a series of jazz musicians were up for the rest of the evening. We drank some, talked and enjoyed the music. After a bit, he asked me if I had a tour of the city, and would I come home with him for a little while. This suave brother had no problem asking for what he wanted, which was fine with me. But I wasn't ready to just dive in with him, so I said yes to the tour but that it was getting too late to go to his place. He smiled once more and led me away for a personal tour that only leads to mischief. We drove around D. C. in his Volvo as he pointed out all the standard tour sights, like the Jefferson Memorial, the Lincoln Memorial, the Mall area, and the Capitol Building. They were all lit up, and I really wanted to go walking around.

I finally asked him about his fancy coat, and he said it was a gift from his boss. I knew he didn't play in a band, but he'd mentioned he was a manager, though I couldn't remember the name of the group. As we went along, Darryl also pointed out little things like the highway, and this and that, and finally, last but not least, brought my private tour to the store on the corner of his street. Hmmm—quite scenic! While we were chatting along, he was navigating and directing with a purpose.

Josephine's Lessons

He left me in the car to go in the store, and when he came out, he handed me a bag as he got in. It was full of Chessman sugar cookies and a box of condoms, given to me as nonchalant as you please. All that and confident too, it seemed! I could tell I was in for a hellova night, and by that point, I was comfortable with and ready for that prospect. He was very attractive. I felt safe with him, and he'd been a downright interesting, fine gentleman all evening. I remember thinking that I could use some good sex tonight, and it would probably be something fairly straightforward. I just didn't get what I expected! Knowing he was about to score with me, Darryl pulled in front of his apartment and led me up the stairs grinning, like he was going to roast the yellow canary and eat him whole.

When we got inside, I saw he had little furniture; however, he had some interesting things, including a table that was from a big, wooden industrial wire roller. He opened the cookies and started munching on the first layer, asking if I wanted to watch a movie. I easily agreed, and he handed me the cookies and cleared the table to set up an old-style, reel projector. He placed director's chairs on either side of the round table, and then he took a film from a drawer and threaded it into the projector. He toyed with the thing for a minute and then faced it onto a clear, white wall in front of us. The film started to play.

It seemed a very different kind of movie, where a group of women were pirates on a ship. The women, all clothed in skimpy pirate bikinis, were sailing home when they captured another ship along the way—a ship that just happened to be full of men with hardly any clothes on. The captive men were pure, movie eye candy; each one an attractive hunk and *fine as hell*. I would have stopped the damn ship, too. I was completely clueless and just watched and enjoyed the scenery, so to speak.

I was lost in thought about silly things like, "Why would a pirate ship have a crew full of women?" Or, "How in the world did those women overtake such beefy guys? They must have used magic." Suddenly, the buxom leader of the pirates pushed this gorgeous hunk of a man to his knees, and ordered him to perform oral sex on her. At last, I realized with a giant, but silent, DUH, that I was being introduced to a porno film! Oh, for heaven's sake! Everything about it suddenly made sense. I was inexperienced about porn, but I didn't want to seem ignorant to Darryl. I kept staring at the movie, and Honey, I was unconsciously gobbling up his Chessman sugar cookies.

Darryl kept watching, too, but the projector was losing its grip on the film, or was starting to jam somehow. Finally, a band of some sort broke, and he tried to fix it with a rubber band. The remainder of the film was lost to us as the quick-fix rubber band kept melting from the heat of the bulb. That was fine with me, as the movie had accomplished its purpose. I was inspired to do something spur-of-the-moment and adventurous, or at least entertaining. I helped Darryl clean off the big round table and told him to put on some music.

The Isley Brothers came crooning out from the bedroom, and I jumped up on the table and got into it, swaying my hips and singing along to "For the Love of You." Darryl pulled up a chair and watched as I sang along, quite off-key, somewhat in time with the song, as I began to strip off my clothes. I was pretty sure my singing wasn't going to be criticized.

Darryl was breathing rather loudly by the time I reached my bra and panties, and I must have finally pushed him over the edge. As he rushed over to the table, he flung me over his shoulder caveman style and headed towards the bedroom. My boobs were bobbing like a buoy against his shoulder. He smelled so good, all excited and acting very, very, masculine! "Excellent," I murmured, as he dropped me on the largest bed I had ever seen. How he managed to get out of his clothes so fast was beyond me. I could not see him when he started, but all of a sudden, I could see that he was naked. Flabbergasted, I laid there and enjoyed the show. He was erect and ready! My, my, my; what a fantastic sight for eyes to behold.

He reached on top of his dresser for a sheath and slipped it on. I had never seen a lambskin condom before, and it fascinated me to see all that hardness enclosed in an animal skin. Almost spellbound, I asked if I could touch it, and he laughed and told me to move fast because soon it was gonna deflate. I gingerly enclosed my hand around him and ooo'd and aah'd at the thinness and feel of it on him. It was almost as if nothing was covering him, and I mentally stored it as another new experience. Now, just how many new experiences I was going to catalogue tonight was yet to be savored.

He took my hands and placed them on my breasts. "Can I be your warrior slave tonight?" he asked. I didn't know what he meant at first, but then he stood me up on the bed and knelt in front of me with his head at my core, like in the pirate movie. He pulled me close to him and ran his tongue all over my sweetness until he found my wondrous bud of glory. And he was excellent at kissing, licking, and tasting me until I couldn't stand up anymore. As I lay down, I said I wasn't a good slave master, and that it was his turn to take charge. He wasted no time and drove into me to show who was going to be the master, and who was going to be the slave.

I practically flew back on the bed from his thrusts being so powerful and so filling. He stroked me and moaned his heavenly chant as we both spiraled into the world of release. All the festivities from earlier in the evening were past, and we got down to the serious business of love making until dawn. I wouldn't have fathomed this rabbit, coat-wearing man would quench me like a fine, exquisite wine. We left his apartment before the sun was up, and the parting breakfast was the last row of the Chessman's.

Lesson learned– When you get invited on a personal tour late at night by a gorgeous hunk of a man, wearing a full-length, rabbit fur coat, be very cautious about going into his burrow. Watching porno movies and enjoying Chessman's, could present you with these sugar cookies as a special breakfast.

12

TIMOTHY – THE AFTER-HOURS MAN

I met Timothy in an after-hour's club operated by my brother and sister in Massachusetts. It was an apartment really, but they had a happening club going, selling drinks and plenty of room for people to dance—which they did into the wee, wee hours of the morning. I was up from college visiting, and they'd asked me to help out at the club that night.

The place was packed full and jumping; it was also quite dark, making it intimate at the same time. I noticed a fine looking man just standing about, and my boldness had me asking him to dance. Timothy said he was waiting on a friend, but he readily agreed after a quick scrutiny of my body, and asked me what a straight girl like me was doing in a joint like this. I explained who my family was, and I suppose that wasn't what he wanted to hear because he kept really quiet while we danced. Timothy was a sexy slow dancer, and we stayed at it for a few songs while building up a good sweat. We were just enjoying ourselves in our own little corner of the club.

After dancing, Timothy gave me his number, and told me if I was ever in town to look him up, and we could hang sometime. With nothing to lose I said, "What about later today?" He smiled and told me where he lived, giving me directions and inviting me to hook up after we got some sleep. He went to find his friend he was waiting for, and they left. I felt fairly impressed with myself and told my sister about the fine young man I had just met. She hadn't noticed because the place was so packed, with minimal lighting, and she'd been plenty busy serving drinks. I was glad she didn't see him first.

Later that evening, I decided to follow up on Timothy's invitation and drove over to his place. The friend I'd seen him with at the club answered the door, and I asked for Timothy. The friend looked at me sort of funny and escorted me through the apartment to a room at the far side of the place. As we went through the living and dining rooms, I noticed several large metal trash cans in the middle of the floor. Odd, but not wanting to seem nosy, I just kept following him quietly. Stranger still, Timothy answered the bedroom door after his friend rapped softly on it, and Timothy pulled me into his bedroom without any greeting at all. There was a bed and another trash can in his room, and that was it. Clothes were thrown here and there, and I was confused because it smelled like fresh cut grass; messy and lonely.

He told me to sit on the bed and wanted to know why I was there. Apparently, he'd forgotten we were getting together today, so I reminded him of our conversation and the directions he'd given me. He made a face and smacked himself on the forehead. Maybe things would get cleared up a bit if I just gave him a minute. "No wonder you came to this address," he said, though I had no idea where else I would have gone.

"I don't really live here, and my friends call me T-Man. When you asked for 'Timothy', they didn't know who you meant. I don't usually invite people here," he explained.

"Sorry, I thought your name was Timothy."

"It is, but c'mon, let's get out of here, and I'll take you someplace to eat."

We ended up at a HoJo's, and during the course of a very pleasant long dinner, we decided to get a room. Looking back, I know now that I never asked the right questions during dinner. All I knew, and all I guess I wanted to know, was that this man was nice, fine looking and successful, which I could tell from his wonderful Lincoln Continental.

Josaphine's Lessons

In the room, Timothy showed me by taking his clothes off first, that *he* wanted to be dessert. I watched him strut around the room making it as cozy as possible. I started to undress, but he stopped my hands and asked could he have the pleasure. I didn't speak, just stared at his every movement. He was graceful and prowling at the same time. I was divested of my clothes slowly, and in an arousing manner, until he had me panting to taste this desirable dessert. We enjoyed each other for hours before he ended the totally, delightfully, sexy dessert-tasting affair. This left me happily glowing as we returned to not-really-his-apartment for my car.

It was the middle of the night when we got back to his place, but folks were still hanging out on the stoops and porches. We went back to his bedroom, and I noticed the large trash cans were gone, replaced by lots of bags of freshly measured marijuana. Nickel and dime bags were everywhere, which explained everything. I was pretty naïve about what I saw, but not *that* stupid. Although it certainly made me uncomfortable, I didn't panic. In spite of the situation I was curious; I actually wanted to know more about what was happening in this place. Timothy went out and talked to his friend for a long time while I was left in the bedroom with the strong, pungent smell of weed. Good thing none of it was lit, or the contact high would be devastating.

After several minutes passed, my happily, sated self was starting to get nervous. All of a sudden, I got thoroughly scared when Timothy burst into the room, knocking me over the other side of the bed and onto the floor. I didn't see stars, but things were spinning a mile a minute as I tried to recover my senses. Timothy flipped the mattress up and took out the biggest gun I had ever seen in my life. It looked like something Dirty Harry would be carrying. He kicked the door shut and told me to be quiet, and I was more than happy to comply. I had no idea what to expect next, but I sure knew this was no longer any kind of ordinary first date. This was an, "Oh shit! What am I doing here?" kind of date. I started to pray and promised all kinds of allegiances if I could come out of this situation without being shot.

My eyes must have been wide as pancakes, but I didn't and couldn't move a muscle. The noise coming from the other rooms was deafening and the waiting was pure hell. Timothy's friend came in and told us to jump out the window because the place was being raided! Shit, shit, shit! Good bye frying pan—hello fire! Everything happened so fast, I couldn't think about what to do next!

Timothy threw open the window, grabbed me like a slap, and then followed his friend out the window. Suddenly, we were running around the building into an alley, then into the back door of another apartment building. I was scared shitless no doubt, but I was keeping up with these grown men because Timothy never let go of my hand.

"Why am I running? I don't know these people! I'm just a college girl visiting a friend," I thought frantically, as I tried to speak audibly.

I finally heard my voice ask Timothy, "Please take me to my car. Please get me out of here!" He looked at me with a face that appeared frightened but pumped up from adrenaline. He led me to another room and asked me to wait a few more minutes before leaving. No one knew where we were and he wanted me to go out unnoticed. He finally apologized for getting me involved in this situation, which pressed me to ask the obvious question, "And just what situation might this be?"

He told me openly that he and his friends ran a joint house, and they were being raided by another drug gang. This gave me pause! No, they weren't being raided by the police. Was this better than being caught by the police—or worse? How could it be worse? Would these other guys still be looking for us? Not knowing the answer, I sat on the floor and waited for what seemed an eternity. Timothy sat next to me and continued to hold my hand. At another place and time, this would have been a rather romantic interlude, like earlier this evening. He told me to get ready to leave and that he was sorry he couldn't walk me back to my car. Too dangerous for him, he explained, as the other gang members would know him, but I could go straight to my car alone safely. I should act like nothing is going on, he coached, and just get into my car, but then I should leave the neighborhood like a blast out of hell. "Oh for heaven's sake! How in the hell am I supposed to walk to my car on wobbly, frightened legs? I'm up to my armpits in this now," I stated intensely. He kissed me goodbye with no mention of ever seeing me again.

With all the courage I could muster, I left for my car and demanded my body to stay calm. How my legs carried me was beyond reasoning. Thankfully, I got to my car without any problems, and then I headed straight to the after-hour's club. To calm my shattered nerves, I had a very large drink and absolutely no dancing and no talking to anybody!

Lesson learned– Anyone met in an after-hour's club is suspicious to start with. There can be no good outcome by dealing with characters met in the dark after midnight. Let it wait until tomorrow. Get some sleep before visiting strange apartments, no matter how good looking the brother might be; you don't want any shooting surprises!

13

BILL – 6'10" OF FANTASY

Growing up in a neighborhood full of people of all sorts has its advantages; the girl's advantages being an assortment of men in all shapes and sizes. Only a few boys in my neighborhood grew as tall as Bill, for instance, so he was an outright standout in the hood.

In high school, he'd been a gangly fellow who'd worn unforgettable bell bottom jeans, creased to a knife point, and so starched they could walk by themselves. After high school and a few wonderful basketball games, he ripened up to his full height of 6'10", making for a nice-looking package. This made approaching him harder for short curvy girls like me. We never got together back then.

One day, many years after high school, I ran into Bill in my usual hang out club. He had that fantastic height, relaxed jeans, and put on a welcoming smile when he saw me. I remembered that he was gangly when we were in school, but this night all I saw was a happy, tall, attractive man who I never really got to know. Alas, an opportunity was sauntering towards me and I loved a challenge of this sort!

I gave Bill an equally warm smile, and he looked as if he would gobble me up. That told me in an instant most of what I needed to know! I asked him if I could buy him a drink, and he said he didn't drink but would take a soda. I finally remembered that about him. I ordered him a soda and a Screwdriver for me, and we sat down to a pleasant, but sexually laced conversation. After a few laughs and reminiscing, I saw that spark in his eyes that told me he wanted a lot more than conversation. I didn't have to wait long. The indication that we were moving towards a common goal came faster than lightning, when he leaned in a little and said, "I have always wanted to be inside your healthy thighs. Do you think I could just taste you once in this lifetime?" He shifted gears so fast I could see my thoughts racing ahead. I was on a third drink thinking maybe my hearing was off. The music was loud, but then he leaned his tall, muscled-up self fully across the tiny table and licked my ear instead of whispering in it.

I sprang up from that table so fast; I toppled it over on him! Thankfully, he laughed it off like it was nothing, and then rescued the situation smooth as you like by asking me to slow dance. Well, we were standing up anyway, so he just slid it all together easily, like a strategic move on the basketball court. He took my hand gently and pulled me close as the music started. I don't remember the song, because I recall my mind being filled to capacity, trying to figure out how this towering hunk and my short, stocky, 5'5" self was going to fit together. I needn't have worried.

The music had us moving just right, swaying against each other in harmony. I must admit that my remaining thoughts were pooling south and enjoying the sensation. Apparently, that swinging and swaying was doing all the work needed, because he bent his head down and said straight into in my ear again, clear as can be, that he wanted to make love to me tonight. Lord, lord, lord! While I had been plotting and planning, Bill was ready to speed things along, right now. I had really been thinking about getting him between the sheets, but his thoughts were quicker.

Decisions, decisions! I could feel a rising, big something, somewhere just under my breast, a *something* that normally would have been a good bit lower, so making a decision was paramount. He was growing more and more excited as we danced. Time to put his words into action.

I stood on my toes trying to talk in his ear and made it to his shoulder to say, "Let's go and get something to eat at the diner." He nodded towards the door and we made our way to the exit. I waved to my friends, and I remembered seeing them chuckle as they watched my short, full-figured, fabulous self, strut out with the tallest, finest, man in the club.

We arrived at the diner and he ordered a burger, fries and a shake while I ordered coffee with sugar, no cream, being careful about the wrong foods before sex. Still buying time, I watched him eat while I peppered him with questions. He told me how much he'd liked me when we were in school but said he didn't have the courage to talk to me then. We ran with different crowds and our paths rarely crossed. Then, we each went away to different colleges, and now here we are, all grown up. "I still want you as badly, and even more so now, than I did back then," he said.

I melted in my chair. The issue of his height seemed to shrink to something manageable when he put his heart on the table like that. He was so open and natural that I didn't think he was jerking me around at all. To Bill, it was time for us to fulfill his teen-hood fantasy. Any resistance I might have couldn't compete with his open-hearted sentiment and sexual determination.

We left the diner and headed to a place he shared with some other basketball players. What a sexy man-filled den of iniquity! We didn't stop to talk at all, but continued straight upstairs to his room.

He had a king-sized bed, of course, and unlike the rest of the place, his room was surprisingly different. I wanted to be there, but I was anxious, excited, and continued to be apprehensive about his height. When I'm uneasy like that, the most idiotic questions can stumble out of my mouth, and tonight that ridiculous trait of mine was in full form. I asked if I was the first person he'd brought up to his room. God, I knew it was dumb the moment I started to say it. It was one of those moments when you wish you could reel it back in.

Without a word, he smiled and sat on the bed pulling me between his thighs. They were strong and tight, long and muscular.

He ignored my dumb chatter, holding me close to kiss me fully and passionately. The room suddenly became very small and damn hot.

Pretty quickly, I broke off the kiss and started to take off my jacket, and he said, "Allow me! This is my fantasy come true." I was hoping he would keep up that sweet smooth talking, and I *know* I was grinning from ear to ear. He was a fantasy of mine, too, he just didn't know it, but he was about to find out!

He removed all my clothes and just looked at me. He was still dressed completely, so I said, "Are you going to take your clothes off?" He stood up and up and up and easily swung me around up onto the bed. Smooth move, too perfect! Standing on the bed, I was finally eye level with him. He kissed me again and I could feel his erection at the right elevation at last. Apparently, he knew this fantasy well and had worked out how to handle this height problem. He released me to disrobe and I fell back on the bed to watch. He removed his clothes with a slowness that had me panting. He started with well-placed kisses on my throat and continued tracing them all over my face and eyes. He finally kissed me full on the mouth and plunged his tongue and finger into my flesh at the same time. My surprised moaning was muffled as he worked majestically making love to my mouth and readiness. I could feel the excitement building with each gentle thrust as he moved his tongue and finger in sync until I started to grind into his hand.

I knew this was going to be sensational when he turned on his back and made me straddle him. As I lifted up, he smoothly put his hardness in me and groaned like he just found a perfect haven. I grabbed onto his shoulders as he sat up a little and told me to do my very best. No further invitation was needed! I rode him slowly at first and then we picked up the tempo. We rode like the devil, without exploding—and slowed, then paused. He pulled me up off his member and kept moving me up, until his face was in contact with me. His mind-blowing fantasy wasn't just in the missionary department. He tasted me like a super-tongued athlete, until I couldn't take anymore without completely losing it. I literally fell over on the bed like a rag doll. He positioned himself on top of me and took my half numb, short legs and pulled them up to his shoulders. That was an amazing feat in itself. He kissed my feet and sucked my toes while he plunged in again and again. We both moaned and groaned out a cataclysmic orgasm that exceeded all expectations. Soon, our releases ended as we toppled in a heap onto the floor. Carpet never felt so good!

I remember lying there, wiped out and sweaty, feeling totally elated. Before passing out, I managed to think how magnificent a fantasy Bill was...so lovely and sweet. After all these years, we finally came together, proving we could both have one hellova fantasy come true!

Lesson learned– Tall men have fantasies about short women all the time. Believe me when I say they will work it out. When lying down, things come into perspective, making new familiarities and fantasies possible. Even if you end up on the carpet.

14

CHUCK – THE DAM MAN

I stopped fooling around in the nightclubs and bars for a while and decided to really get into my job. I was teaching at the time and wanted to realize "peace of mind." Everything was going boringly fine, until the day I received dreadful news of my very dear friend being just minutes from her death bed. I needed something or someone to comfort and soothe me. I should have remembered the saying, "be careful what you wish for."

My friend knew she was dying, and wanted to see me for what we knew would be the last time. The visit scared me completely. After leaving her room, I was determined not to drink myself into oblivion, so I made an out-of-the-way trip to an all-night bookstore in another town. This gave me time to think and go over in my mind how the visit had gone, and to calm down.

It had been earth shattering to see her like that, and I felt at sea, without anything solid or comforting to hold onto, while I swayed to the rolling waves. The bookstore had a café and made a good, all night hang-out. It offered great books, magazines, coffee, and different types of cakes to keep you happily reading and eating. It was a great way to drown out the world! As I headed into the café for coffee and triple layer chocolate cake, I saw a guy I knew from my town reading magazines. He was completely absorbed and I sailed on past, lost in my own thoughts of my ill friend.

Chocolate always tops the list for comforting me, and if it is in cake form, well—I'm in heaven and the distraction can be completed. I sat down in one of the love seat arrangements and put the first taste of cake in my mouth. It was so rich, creamy, and moist that I moaned from the pure enjoyment of the taste. I apparently did it really loud, because the guy I recognized looked up and headed my way with a passion-filled grin on his face.

He asked if he could sit down, and then asked me if my name was Josaphine. I said yes, and asked, when we had been introduced, and why I recognized him. We discovered we had many mutual friends and frequented the same clubs and restaurants. I wondered to myself, with so many similar connections, why we'd never crossed paths before. He asked me if I came to this bookstore a lot, and I said that I went to college not far from here. He asked if we could come together sometime to the bookstore, and I readily agreed. I wanted to get to know him better in all areas.

We laughed and talked for a very soothing and distracting hour or so. When I stood to leave, he asked to follow me home to make sure I got there safely. Impressed, I said of course, and he followed me back to town. He walked me to the door and asked what I was doing the next day. I had no plans and was open to whatever he might suggest. He asked if I could swim, and I said yes—but not very well. Chuck assured me that floating was all that was needed, and we agreed to hook up the next day for a mystery swim date.

The next morning as I ate breakfast, I thought about my time with Chuck and found myself thankful he'd been there, helping me to calm down. I truly enjoyed his company. The phone rang then, and it was Chuck saying he was on his way. I had just enough time to squeeze into my sexy, black, backless bathing suit.

The swimsuit was a treat after my first paycheck and months later, I was finally going to wear it. Chuck drove us to a park and then walked me into a small forest and up a trail that seemed endless. He assured me the hike was worth it. I wished I had worn more durable sandals instead of the cute little ones I had on. I would ask him to rub my feet when we stopped, which I was sure must be over this next hill.

When we got past the top and started down another trail, the sight was spectacular, worth every bit of effort. Chuck paused with me as we looked out over a story-book scenic lake, with a bridge that crossed over a small dam. I lived in this city all my life and never knew this side of the lake was here. Chuck had grown up near the lake with the dam on this side, and it was one of his favorite spots to relax.

He remembered the tension I had the night before and wanted to show me the healing powers a place like this could have. I thought that was so sweet, but my mischief-loving side jumped in. "The lake is nice and all, but I could use your body to take some tension away!" I just up and said it out loud, bold as you please.

Instantly, he had that passion-filled grin on his face again. I laughed, but when he took his shirt off, all my laughter quickly vanished, and I swore to the heavens that I was going to take advantage of this lusty mess of muscles. What is a horny, sexy, full-figured, black woman supposed to do in a situation like this anyway?

As soon as we'd gotten down to our swimsuits, he led me down the slope to a spot where the shore was up under some trees. As pretty as it was, I was a little nervous, and I asked if it was safe to swim here. He took my hand, and reassured me we'd be okay. His confidence was contagious, and I settled enough to notice how gorgeous and strong he was with that good looking hair. He was marvelous to look at from the top of his head down to his manly toes. Also, his calm, take-charge attitude soothed me quickly with hardly a word spoken.

We dove into the water and it was freezing! I could feel my nipples harden on impact. Gorgeous, as it was, my swimsuit wasn't going to hide anything. We swam away from the shore to the middle of the lake. I stopped, treading water to catch my breath. I noticed Chuck was completely at ease, not winded in the least. I asked if he swam daily, and he said his visits weren't as frequent as when he was a boy.

He was far from being a boy now, and he was delicious scenery to take in. His arms moved smoothly through the water as he hovered near me, and he asked if I could float. I laughed and said, "I probably float better than I swim." Chuck came closer, turned me around, and had me lay on my back between his legs, while he swam backwards towards the bridge.

He was still able to talk calmly, but I was getting more and more apprehensive. He felt so good beneath me, and was just so sweet and sexy, but I couldn't see where we were going. We reached the bridge and he pushed me up onto the narrow cement walkway. As we looked over the other side, he told me that the lake drops forty-four feet to the water below. He told me that he and his brothers used to jump off the bridge and swim across to the park shore. That was a long way down, and a long way to go, but even though I felt scared, I was thinking about how to do it. Not wanting to be any sort of chicken I asked, "Do you want to jump?" "Only if you come with me!" he said, and took my hand leading me over the fence to perch on the side of the drop.

When we climbed over, I knew I had truly lost my mind. Fear crashed in as I started figuring out what I was doing. What in heaven's name was I thinking? But there was no going back as he took my hand and said, "Let's do it now! JUMP!"

I remember falling, falling, and more falling together, the water still too far away. I don't remember whether I screamed or not. When we hit the water he let me go, and I could tell we went deep. Eyes closed, I tried to spring back up, but I never reached any bottom to push off of. Finally, I opened my eyes and saw Chuck's feet above me as he swam to the surface. It seemed too far away and I already felt exhausted before the jump. I remember my heart pounding for all it was worth and my ears hurting from the pressure. Chuck reached the surface and plunged his hand in to draw me up the final few feet. Honey, I clung to him for dear life. But, oh! What a rush!

When I felt his hands on my breast, turning me away from him, I realized I had lost my bathing suit! I was naked and so was he. Our swimsuits hadn't come off from the jump; they came off from shooting back up so fast. We stayed steady together with my back pressed against him treading water, for a few moments. Hungrily, he turned me around and kissed me full on the mouth, tongue and all!

What can he be thinking? Doesn't he know I need to breathe? My worries left me as he wrapped my legs around his waist and told me to hold on. We stayed together like that as he pulled us along and hit the wall. Next, he was putting my hands on a safety rope behind me that was attached to the dam. As I held on tight, he dove down under the water, and then came up against my body to flatten us to the wall. I didn't know what to expect, but somehow I was penetrated with his erection pushed inside me, and I squeezed back for all I was worth.

He was doing one hellova balancing act, pushing into me, when I let go of the rope with one hand to hold onto his broad shoulders. Even Chuck had his limits, though, and he told me to hold on to the rope because he couldn't hold us both up. He was strong and hard everywhere, using it to full effect! He pushed and pushed and pushed, and I matched every thrust. When I was ready to come, I felt a scream on the tip of my tongue, ready to let loose. Chuck pulled my legs up farther around his waist and I tried to kiss my orgasm into him as I clamped on. He finally released within me as his tongue burst into my mouth. I was totally exhausted, and as I recovered from all that exertion, I didn't know how I was going to swim to the park shore. I thought we were stranded for a moment, and then Chuck told me to release my hands and just drop into the water. I said, "Oh, hell no!" I was too scared to even think about it, much less actually let go. I remember thinking I couldn't stand up even if I was on solid ground, so how could he expect me to swim after such amazing sexual exertion? He promised he would catch me and not let me go under. With him, I dropped into the water, and then he turned on his back again and placed me between his thighs as he backstroked down the water away from the dam to the shore. I finally relaxed into it and let him carry me, feeling the sunshine on my naked body and the warmth of his body underneath. The water was soothing, comforting and my fears completely dissolved as I soaked up the quietness, too. I was so calm; I never gave a second thought about losing my new swimsuit....

Lesson learned– Sometimes the oddest situations will come your way to comfort and sooth you when you need it most. Just trust your instincts and the warm hands holding you when it's time to jump into the deep water. Your friend will be there swimming under you and enticing you to do many other things to release tension in your body—much better than eating three-layer chocolate cake. DAM!

15

BUTCH – WORK WITH IT

There was a time, most particularly a long stretch one year, when I thought having sex was really the most important thing in my life. Some readers might have a name for a person like that, and some might say, I just hadn't found the right person to settle down with yet. I suppose I needed to do more body searching. Either way, that's just the way I felt at the time. For a while, I honed my skills, watched who was interested in my skirts, and searched around every chance I could get!

The bar scene was a favorite place to hang out, and it certainly suited my lifestyle at the moment. There were several great bars close to one another. It seemed a bit like grazing through fields of attractive places to drink and mix. If I didn't find anyone to hang out with for the night in one bar or club, I would simply finish my drink and head to the next place with or without my friends.

One night, I was on the third establishment of the evening, and getting antsy for something good to happen. At times, you can spot what you need quickly, and my eye zeroed in on a friend I hadn't seen for a while coming through the door. He saw me right away and waved, walking towards me swaying his hips which made for an interesting swagger. I thought for a moment how nice looking Butch was and immediately felt a tiny a bit guilty.

Butch was a longtime friend, and I had dated one of his relatives. He was more a brother- type of friend than anything. Looking at him that way felt strange, but I had to remind myself that he was definitely not off limits. We had a drink or two to get reacquainted before he asked me to dance. Dancing was always an intimate weakness in life for me, and I agreed eagerly. We were quickly surrounded by many couples on the floor grinding to the rhythm of a sweet, slow song. Glancing around in the dimness, I could see several couples kissing softly. Butch bent his lips toward mine, but I hesitated briefly before engaging in a small peck on his lips. I still felt awkward concerning my thoughts for him, and he laughed and held me tighter and kissed me gently on the side of my neck. Surprisingly, it sent shivers down my body, a signal he sensed immediately. He didn't waste any time and whispered in my ear, "Shall we go to your place?" Reluctant and uncertain, I remembered my purpose, and we headed for the door. He didn't have a car, so we left together in mine.

When we arrived at my townhouse, it looked like my roommates were out for the evening. He asked if I had anything to drink, so I poured us both a shot of Jack Daniels. He sipped his drink, and motioned for me to follow him to my living room area. I was happy for him to lead. He placed an album on the stereo and pulled me against him gently, and started a very sensual slow dance. We were going to pick up where we left off at the club, apparently.

I felt so mellow and relaxed that it was completely natural to turn up the seduction, as I swayed my hips provocatively against him. I must have made the signal as strong as it could be, because he stopped dancing, studied me, and decided straight away to lead me upstairs to my bedroom. I followed him and went along, but for some reason, all the while in the back of mind, I was thinking, "This is Butch—and this could be a bad, a very bad idea!"

In his opinion, Butch thought it was a fine idea, and worked to show me how much. I deliberately said to myself, perhaps I could set aside my apprehensions long enough to have a good time. Butch closed my bedroom door, and started to undress me. He was very gentle, and it made me think of how he'd been sweet and easy with me the whole night. Also, it made me think, that as long as I'd known him, he was always sweet. Too sweet, if you get my drift! Now, on the other side of the coin, I was thinking, maybe we should have been together before this night, and perhaps I'd been missing out on something good all along!

He seated me on the bed and dropped to the floor to remove my boots, showing me some additional romance. I had been undressed many times, and nothing I'd done until now seemed as smooth and gentle with his touch. He stood me up and removed my turtle neck and unzipped the back of my wool skirt, letting it fall to the floor. The silk lining made a soft, whooshing sound down my stocking-covered legs. He took my hands and I stepped out of the skirt. He carefully folded it onto the chair with my sweater and joined me again to remove my tights.

Instead of feeling cooler out of my clothes, somehow the temperature was warming. I remained very still and let the anticipation slowly come over me, because this smooth fingered man had revved up my body and wrapped up my emotions all together. I was ready to rock our world all night, but he still took it nice and easy, a crucial, one step at a time.

The music we had on wasn't appropriate for the occasion, so, I reached for the tape player on my night stand, and put on some slow dancing music. With a little grin, Butch began to grind his hips into the air. I was a happy audience as he began to sway back and forth, taking his sweater off. His chest was nicely shaped, not overly muscled and surprising hairless. My mind was asking if he waxed his chest. He reached for his pants and undid the belt, then the button and zipper. I was becoming even more impatient! He took off his pants, walked to the light and turned it off. Damn, I wished he was totally naked before the lights went out. Did I spot boxers under those pants?

He joined me on the bed, and I whispered for him to remove the rest of my clothes. He placed me in front of him facing into the bed, unclasped my bra and reached around me, to gently massage my breast. He tugged my panties down, and I lifted up for him to remove them. I tried to turn around, but he wouldn't let me, and he began to lick slowly down my spine. Going slow had me overheating and pulsating on the brink of getting ready to be violent! I was literally shaking! I pushed back against him, and just then realized I probably outweighed him by fifty or sixty pounds. Advantage, Josaphine! I turned around and wrestled him down, rolled on top and got into it! He complied happily, though I knew he really had no choice, and I pulled off his underwear, and then swung them over my head in victory.

This was my game now, smoothness and gentleness be damned. I touched his thigh and realized I wanted to see what's in store for me. I reached for the lamp, and turned it on and he lay completely still. I looked at him and he smiled and said, "Honey, this is what I got, you'll just have to work with it!"

Lesson learned– If you are feeling guilty and it seems like a bad idea in the back of your mind, listen; because, maybe it really is. Being over anxious and impatient can surprise you with a reality of having to just "work with it!"

16

ZEKE – THE SECOND WHITE GUY

During a blizzard, there are many things apartment building neighbors do to help each other out. In 1978, we had a terrible blizzard that swept the New England states. As the storm was really getting under way, I drove home from my job with the necessary "letter B" items needed to survive: I had bags of bread, breakfast, bologna, butter, batteries, booze and beer. My neighbor across from me on the first floor helped me bring in the groceries.

My roommate had not gotten home yet, but I didn't start to worry. Snow was coming down heavily, but it was just beginning to pile up. My neighbor said she hadn't been able to get to the store and worse, she had company that didn't look like they were going to be able to leave in time to beat the storm. Being the good neighbor, I suggested we pull our resources together and have dinner, then play some games and make the best of things. She said she would bring blizzard dessert and headed back into her apartment.

Our storm dinner made for an interesting, unplanned affair with two black women, four white guys, and one white woman. During the time it took to cook, eat and laugh uncontrollably for three hours, we got comfortable and learned a great deal about each other. Some of us, including me, played double-deck Pinochle quite well, and to pass the time, we laid down the challenges and house rules. My neighbor, her boyfriend and brother watched a VHS tape in the living room.

Two of the white guys were friends of my neighbor's boyfriend, and maybe in their early forties; very out of their normal comfort zone. Nevertheless, they made themselves at home and set down a challenge to me and my roommate, threatening to spank our asses with a bit of bravado. It was a massacre, but we did the cleaning up! They'd walked into a baited trap with us and didn't know what hit them.

After brutally taking them for three games in a row, moving us late, later and latest into the night, those poor guys were too tipsy and tired to keep up the challenge. My neighbor and her boyfriend took their beaten comrades back to her apartment to lick their wounds, but with a lot of guts, they demanded a rematch later in the day.

It was almost dawn by then. We could see a constant flurry of heavy snow and heard the nearly nonstop shrieking wind of the unforgiving blizzard. We knew no one would be coming and going for at least a couple days and even then, there'd be a lot of snow shoveling work. We might be playing a whole lot of damn cards. I better pace myself....

After laughing with my roommate and saying good night, I headed off to my room. I brushed my teeth, washed my face, and was so ready for bed; I didn't even bother to turn on the light. I could see my sheets and blankets all crumpled up, and thought I had forgotten to make my bed yesterday. That's what was going through my mind when I saw a long, white male hand resting on my pillow in the moonlight.

I nearly wanted to scream, but I caught myself. I knew no one had come in through my balcony doors or through the house to get there. It had to be...hmmmmm!!!

I tiptoed to the bed and yanked the covers back to reveal a long, very masculine, sexy, naked white guy lying on his stomach. Well, ok, this was a pleasant sight, and trailed my eyes up and down the scenery as they adjusted to the darkness. He had the nicest ass! It was pure, tight, vanilla ice cream mounds. I don't know why the sight made me realize it was my neighbor's brother, Zeke; obviously, he didn't watch the entire movie, and this was why. He had found his way to my room and had fallen asleep trying to surprise me, I supposed!

I sniffed, and discovered he had showered, too. "Well, damn," I thought, "he smells good, fresh, and that white creamy frame looks absolutely delicious, all laid out on my nice red sheets." I was mesmerized, enjoying the view, and he was somewhat awake. He slowly turned over reaching for the covers, and laid his palm on my boobs in the process. He never opened his eyes but began to feel and rub them saying purely by braille, "Hello there puppies!" He made me laugh out loud. "I know your ass ain't sleeping!" I whispered.

He chuckled deep in his throat, sounding like a bear's sleepy growl. He pulled me down on top of him with all my clothes on and pulled the covers over us. "Catastrophe or just another very bad idea?" I asked myself. I began to hug him. I had to admit, he was fine, fine, fine. A real womanizer to take me and my room for granted like that, and sneak right into my bed between the sheets. But for now, well, here he was—in my sheets. Lord Jesus! What's a proper black woman to do?

I was plenty tired; tired enough that I just went with it, and let the thrill move things along. I closed my eyes and kissed him. After few mind boggling kisses, it was clear to me that this was absolutely the right choice, and I kissed on him like a woman who had a purpose. Next thing I knew, he woke enough to massage my clothes right off me and threw them on the floor. Sunlight was beginning to dance through my balcony windows, when he asked if he could make love to me all morning.

Good God Almighty, this has to be some kind of record for the fastest foreplay yet! I was in trouble and caving in to the yummy, tempting treat. He felt so good lying there with his arms wrapped around me, and there was no way I was letting go of my most excellent find. I said "yes," but I told him I had a very important rematch game to play around noon, and he would need to be finished by then.

He began to tease me and please me. Somehow I don't think a time limit mattered to him at the moment.

He slid his hand down my thighs and up the inside, gently rubbing and drawing circles with his palm. In record time, I was ready to fly, and I trembled and shook in ecstasy like I'd been missing it. I moaned and groaned nonstop from the time he entered me until I passed out in a fit of spastic glory, with all the special effects, including me hearing the choir singing "Hallelujah!" I could feel my eyes, lips, cheeks, and pretty much every other part of my body, grinning as I fell fast asleep.

Lesson learned– In a blizzard, pull together all your resources that begin with the letter "B" items. Keep clean sheets on your bed, and be ready to help those folks that may need to sleep over. In a blizzard it's simple: all bets are on and there are no "house rules for bedroom games."

17

TOM – THE THIRD WHITE GUY

I cracked my eyes and saw the ceiling of the tent I was occupying with four other people. It was freezing cold outside, white with twenty-four inches of fresh snow in the Capitan Mountains. I was on an adventure expedition, and though I could see how the term "adventure" might find its way into a brochure, for the life of me I didn't know how anyone found this fun or exciting. I was freezing my ass off and hungry. In four words, "absolutely out of place!"

All I had eaten in the days as we climbed the mountain and crossed fields of snow, were some berries, an energy bar, and water. I was hungry, just hungry, to the point where I almost didn't think about the cold. After dinner, inside my down sleeping bag were my clothes, hiking boots and wool socks—one pair still on my feet—plus my down jacket, and wool gloves. I had a wool balaclava hat on my head, and the sleeping bag was zipped all around me mummy style. I chuckled miserably to myself, thinking that if my friends could see me now, they would not believe that Josaphine, the full-figured, citified black woman was in a tent full of white folks, stuck out in deep snow.

I chuckled again as I thought how odd it was that somehow I was chosen as the fifth person in this tent, while the others had groups of four. I wondered in particular why that good looking, mountain guide put me in here with him. Hmmmm....

I had to admit that our guide, Tom, was a tasty looking white guy. He was over six feet tall, had reddish brown hair, and long strong arms that helped me over rocks and snow mounds. He had wonderful, piercing green eyes. His delicious red mustache and beard covered smooth, baby-looking skin with scattered freckles. He was good dream material to focus on as I drifted off to sleep in this really cold tent.

"Hey, wake up; it's time to get dressed! We've got to climb up to our next site," said Tom. I just rolled over and went back to sleep with a deep sigh. I wasn't ready to move to the next anything. Whatever *it* is could come to me for all I cared. I was too damned cold, too sleepy headed. I tried to move my lips and say so, but nothing came out but whines that might have sounded like "go the hell away." His annoying voice, however, kept on calling my name, and asking me to get up again, and again, and again, like a broken too-early-in-the-morning record. Finally, I managed to rub my eyes and attempted a squinty look. I could see enough to know that everyone but me was on their feet getting dressed, carefully nudging about in the cramped space.

I tried to roll over against the tent wall and escape, but there wasn't enough room to get away. I felt someone yanking on the zipper of my sleeping bag, and that got my attention as I swore profusely at them, sight unseen. Tom burst into a fit of laughter, and promised to wash my mouth out with snow if I didn't get my ass moving. I forgot all that because I was still half in dream land, and went immediately back to the previous night's fantasy of Tom's hands on my body. The pure ecstasy of it made me moan, and I tried to roll over and get away again. Snuggle, snuggle, snuggle. All you people go away, and let me dream some more.

I heard that the best way to keep warm was to sleep naked in your bag, so somehow during the night, I had shaken off my wool long johns and was as naked as a jay bird. It worked, too. I was nice and toasty. Tom, however, wasn't going away and was waiting for me to get up. He soon dropped down by me again to unfasten my sleeping bag. I looked at him and asked, "Do you know what I'm wearing

Josaphine's Lessons

in this bag?" That image stopped him. But he didn't jump back and instead, persistent pest that he was, asked if I had any clothes on?

"And wouldn't you just like to find out?" I asked through my sleepy eyes. I was genuinely determined to either get some more sleep or get back to the dream I'd been having, in the flesh. One way or another, dammit, I'm going to get some heated satisfaction before I got out in the cold again.

The rest of the crew was already out milling about the campsite getting coffee, some breakfast, and getting ready to hike. Tom stood up and yelled out the flap to the crew to go on without us because I wasn't feeling well, and he had to look after me for a while. I could hear a few responses from folks that were concerned, but one of the most seriously concerned parties was me! I struggled to wake up enough to grasp what was going on, and I know I had a thoroughly puzzled look on my face when he turned back to me.

He zipped the tent closed and turned to me and smiled saying, "If you wanted to sleep in, I am going to show you how to keep really warm in a sleeping bag." I stared, thinking, OH, I went and really did it, didn't I. This time, with another white guy built like a bear, and a fine-ass guide, to boot! "Maybe, this is not the best idea," I said. But when Tom took off his wool shirt, and sat down to undo his Fabiano's, I was getting rather warm in that bag without any assistance at all!

He didn't bother with sweet nothings in my ear; he was purpose-bound to get in my bag and lay next to me without any delay. He was in that bag quicker than I expected, and jumped right on top of me while zipping the bag reclosed. I was truly amazed at his dexterity and how comfortably we fit in my sleeping bag.

He broke the silence by asking me profound questions that must have lingered in his mind, until this so-called, "perfect opportunity" happened. "Is it true what they say about black women? Is it really the blacker the berry, the sweeter the juice?" But that was all the conversation he was giving, as he proceeded to taste the juice in my mouth with a power-packed kiss.

I was kissed again, fondled, touched and tasted until I felt nearly senseless and really worn out! Tom found ways to get into sexual positions in a sleeping bag that seemed hardly possible, and I would have to say some of them were probably outlawed in some parts of the country. He harvested not only some sweet juice, but also a truckload of curvy, black, Josaphine berries as a result of his inspired *treatment* "for my not feeling good."

We climaxed so hard the zipper ripped open, exposing us to the cold morning and providing a moment of comic relief in the midst of our passion. Nonetheless, I was a happy, hot, and fully "recovered" camper, totally ready to return to sleep in a much better condition. I slid into a nice oblivion.... "Wake up!" Tom shouted, breaking me out of a dead sleep. "You have five minutes now to pack your gear. Come on! You've got to get ready so we can hike to the next campsite! Let's get a move on, city girl!"

I fully woke up and looked around but saw no one inside the tent. I reached across myself to scratch my arms, and all the wrong places, where my wool long johns were irritating me. I shimmied out into what was still a freezing cold morning, hungry as ever, plus, also frustrated that I had missed hot coffee with breakfast. Damn if I didn't have to pee, which done out in the cold didn't seem all that easy or pleasing. I got dressed on the double. The rest of the group was packing up their tents and gear, and I was still wrestling with the sight of Tom. The man was too fine for his own good. Well, I knew better than to dream a fantasy about him. It's going to be a long, rest of the trip. Perhaps there will come a time when I might get arrested for once again trying out those unlawful positions in a sleeping bag. Unfortunately, Tom was all business as usual for the rest of this camping trip.

Lesson learned– Don't sleep in the same tent with the sexy guide, if you can help it. If you are ready, willing, and able to prove the saying, "the blacker the berry, the sweeter the juice," this should happen only in your dreams. Contemplating an unlawful, sexual tryst with the guide could have you colder than usual and without morning coffee.

18

DON – THE FOURTH WHITE GUY

I spent some time in the Midwest at summer school, and the whole experience was a great eye-opener. Never in my life had I seen men as large as those "farm fed white boys!" Seeing all those huge, white guys rearranged my entire sense of sports. Everywhere I turned and whatever the game, big, beefy white hunks were there and I enjoyed the view! Early on after arriving, I had no idea that I'd get to fulfill a bit of local fantasy....

I'd been asked to care for an apartment for one of the deans. It was small, with a galley kitchen, two small bedrooms, a dining area, and a cozy living room. It had two bathrooms, but they were so tiny, they could really only fit one person at a time. The place was entirely suited for my purposes, and I appreciated it.

One day, I went to the cafeteria because the apartment was running on empty. I probably would have gone out even if I'd had something decent to fix though, because it was too hot to cook in such a small space. I met up with a girlfriend at the cafeteria and invited her to come over to watch TV. She was delighted and asked if she could bring a friend. I didn't see any real problem with that, but because it was the dean's place, I asked that she be discreet.

She arrived around 8:00 p.m. and her boyfriend arrived about twenty minutes later. He had to run an errand and when he arrived, he wasn't alone. He managed to pick up a straggler named Don. By sheer coincidence, Don and I had a history. Not long before that night, he agreed to let me catch him during a Sadie Hawkins race, but I was a slow runner and he was quickly gone. I couldn't find him anywhere, and I wondered how much he really "agreed" to let me catch him!

It hadn't really meant anything, and Don and I had each gone to the dance with someone else. We'd spoken occasionally since then, but hadn't gone so far as to make a date, at least not until that point.

My friend and her man took the love seat and I sat next to Don on the couch, which was no hardship at all! I was attracted to him and he was easy on the eyes. He was a tall, hunky, Midwestern white boy with sandy blonde hair, straight white teeth, a killer smile, and the bluest eyes I had ever seen. He looked like a cowboy, broad shouldered and a bit bow legged. I recalled that he made a perfect picture on a horse, and I remembered thinking he could wear the hell out of a cowboy hat, too. Basically, in my book, he was damned fine, just from a different world than me.

I made some drinks, Jack Daniels and Budweiser, good, old-fashioned boilermakers, to lubricate the evening. We had a great time talking and laughing and ended up not watching much TV. Over the course of the evening, my friend and her beau started snuggling and kissing more and more, finally getting hot and heavy enough that they decided they needed to go. I couldn't blame her; however, that left me slightly tipsy and alone with Don.

After seeing my friends to the door, I sat down next to Don and he reached out to kiss me. He was extremely attractive but he had these skinny little lips, which suddenly became something to consider. I wasn't sure how that would feel against my full-figured ones, but I was willing to find out.

I guess I had been staring, as my tipsy mind was calculating that, because he stopped just before contact and asked me to close my eyes, kissing one eye and then the other. He gently kissed my left cheek, then the right before he planted a wet kiss right on my lips. His explorations were entirely successful, and I parted my mouth so he could plunge his tongue in, which he did faster than a rodeo cowboy could rope a calf.

We tangled like that for a few minutes when the apartment began to feel hot, way too hot. I was ready to strip my clothes off and get naked on the floor. He could see my desire and asked if I wanted to go all the way. I said, "What, are we in high school? I thought we already were!" Don smiled that killer smile again and took my hands to lead me down the hall to one of the bedrooms. Since I was so hot, I turned the thermostat down as far as it would go to chill the apartment, and then suggested I freshen up with a quick shower. He wanted to join me, but that bathroom was not designed for foreplay. That was a shame! I would have loved to soap up his body, and I told him so as I ducked into the shower. As he showered after me, I went to jump in the bed, discovering along the way that I'd made the room too cold. My nipples were definitely at attention.

The situation made me think of a Goldie Locks and three-bear's routine, so I got a down comforter, lit some candles, put on some soft music and got in bed. I immediately began to get toasty all over, finding the just right Goldie Locks balance. Don came out of the shower naked and wet, glistening in the candlelight. The setting was just right, indeed, and I thought the ambiance was conducive to lovemaking all night. I was practically tingling with excitement. I was going to enjoy my big wet, athletic, white cowboy hunk! He walked slowly towards the bed, and I asked him to turn around for me. I lustfully took my fill of his body and reached to pull him into bed. As he got closer, I felt a little guilty, as I noticed his member had shriveled in the cold room. He climbed under the covers and as soon as he came close, I realized I had turned this poor guy into a block of ice! I didn't want him to touch me until he warmed up, especially with those big, ice cube feet.

He didn't have to complain for me to know the problem, but he asked me to massage his chest so he could warm up under the blankets. I happily complied, telling him I'd get him completely warmed up and comfy, and began to massage his chest, his stomach, his belly button, his pubic region and finally, I began to stroke and rub his manhood. Warm and comfy, indeed! I felt it lengthen in my hand as he responded to my treatments, becoming velvety nice, stiff, and long. The iceberg was melting, and I anticipated the moment when he would enter me, and I would scream from the enjoyment. He kissed me all over as I rubbed and stroked his hardness, and quickly, he couldn't withstand my caresses any more, mounting ready to take me.

Swiftly, this was going too fast, and I blurted out my warning that he could not come inside me, because we didn't use a love glove. By the time I had managed to utter those words though, my big, robust cowboy stud had entered me, pushing deeply, climaxing and was already leaving the rodeo. I was just floored, flabbergasted, astonished! I don't remember what words actually made it past my lips, but I recall that all I could do inside my head was stutter a series of "But, hell, shit, wait! I wanted to ride, too!" I focused on him and watched my dreamy fantasy dissolve.

While I was swearing silently in shock, Don rolled over without looking at me, asking me to give him a minute while he regained some more momentum, so the party could resume. He was asleep in seconds, because the cowboy had had his final fireworks for the night.

Lesson learned– If he runs fast, drinks fast, ropes a calf fast and kisses fast, you can pretty much guarantee he will do everything else fast, too.

19

WILL – JUST FRIENDS

There comes a time when you think the man of your dreams has entered your life. I thought Will was such a man for me. He was everything I wanted; conservative, tall, darker than me and definitely quieter than me. He was nicely built and had a great confident air about him. Overall, he looked fabulous, and as the song says, "he was too sexy for his shirt."

We worked together on a project that lasted almost a year with several other employees at work. When I first found out he would be one of the participants, my heart did back flips. I put myself in every possible situation to be near him and to work even closer. I had a major crush, even though I was almost thirty! The problem, of course, was that I had no idea what he thought of me. For the longest time nothing happened, and I was becoming utterly disheartened about my prospects with him, but my crush kept crushing. Every time I was around him, I didn't need any heat to make me flare!

One day near the end of our project, we were meeting as a team in a lovely conference resort, and again I wished and wished for the opportunity to be alone with him. During the previous nine months the project had gone smoothly, and I thought our relationship was building, too. I still felt it wasn't going fast enough for me, and I was on the lookout for my chances.

We worked closely for many nights together at the conference center, and one night, we took a stroll through the lobby, laughing and talking comfortably until we were outside between buildings. We found a deserted room, which was a library and lounge with a lit fireplace, to continue talking. We sat down on a fluffy throw rug, and at long last he reached for me. He took my hand and started to rub my fingers. That simple gesture was the cream on top for me as I dreamily looked into his eyes and smiled.

I nearly giggled like a teenager, but I didn't want to send him running for the hills. He reached behind my head and brought my face closer to his. He said quietly that he was going to kiss me, and if I wanted to leave before he did that, I could. What incredible nonsense I thought; I wouldn't have moved if an earthquake had hit.

He kissed me gently and I, of course, parted my lips. He expertly probed around in my mouth in a very sexual manner, sending me into total bliss. My head was doing all kinds of flips and flops, and then he pulled me closer and leaned back down on the rug, pulling me with him to the floor and never breaking our kiss. He'd passed my "kiss test" with a perfect A+, and I was definitely in heaven. We were past the "Big Hurdle," and I thought nothing could go wrong. I was ready to lay there and kiss him until the sun came up.

He broke our kiss for a moment and asked me to stay put as he returned to the door and locked it. I was thinking, "Yeah, boy, you go," until I realized he might want to go further than kissing, first date or not. He took off his sweater and shoes and I did the same. When he sat back down again, I saw him unbuttoning his shirt. The firelight danced lazily across his face and chest. I immediately wanted to kiss every inch of him. He reached for me again and asked if I knew what he wanted to do. Hmmm!

Nothing was hard to figure out at that point. He asked me if he could make love to me right there. My heart was already lost and I didn't know if I wanted it found or not. He unbuttoned my blouse and then unhooked my bra. I had to take a deep breath and told myself to remember to breathe. I was there with the love of my life, the man of my dreams, and I think he knew it pretty clearly. Every touch stoked my passion, and I know I moaned and groaned as though I was insane.

He kissed one nipple, then the other and down my breast to my stomach, to my belly button. He wanted to go further but was hindered by my pants. He deftly removed them and my panties, and began to kiss me over and over again. When he finally kissed the juncture of my thighs, my lights went out, replaced by a new awareness of fire entering my body. His tongue was a blazing torch, hot and sizzling inside me. I didn't simply orgasm, but clenched so hard over and over that I truly and actually passed out, taken beyond exhilaration!

When I came to my senses, I was in my room under the covers, unfortunately alone. My roommate for the conference had returned and was talking too fast for my brain to wrap around any sentence. She and several members of our group were partying in the resort's nightclub until the wee hours, and would I care to come along? I hated to miss that party, but I felt drained and happy, remembering the party of my own I'd just attended. Hell, I was still too drunk with the ecstasy to remember how I'd gotten to my room!

Later that day we all returned to our prospective homes, and though I looked for him, I didn't see Will, nor could I reach him for two days, even though we worked in the same office. How could I face him after what had happened? I resolved to be brave and tell him I wanted to see more of him because I had strong feelings for him. I rehearsed what I would say and set out in search of him, but no one had seen him since the conference ended.

I began to worry! I remember thinking maybe he had been in an accident. I had his home number and called his house. No answer. I was sick with worry for the rest of the day. The next two days crept by and still no word. Our wonderful rendezvous was becoming a misty memory, and I was worried sick. At last, four days after our encounter, my phone rang and it was Will. He wanted to come to my house that night, right away, because he wanted to talk to me.

I had two female roommates, who were fully aware of my passionate desire for Will. I raced home to get ready for a big night and unceremoniously kicked my roommates out to go to a movie. Then the doorbell rang. Will came in with a bottle of Jack Daniels and a six-pack of Budweiser, my favorite boilermaker ingredients. I smiled and accepted his gifts as he came in, and sat in a chair facing the couch. When I returned from the kitchen with drinks, he wasted no time in asking me to sit down. I was primed to set my script in motion, but something seemed somehow out of kilter with him, so I hung back, waiting. I sat across from him and he began talking like we were just friends and coworkers. He told me that since the conference he'd been out of the office in part because of me.

He said he knew I was in love with him. This wasn't sounding right at all, and I started to get that sort of tunnel vision that comes on when you know things aren't right.... It seemed Will was reciting from his own script; he calmly and quietly told me with regret that he was now engaged to another woman, someone on the project with us!

I could hardly breathe. I was so shocked! I hadn't even known they liked each other at all, much less that they'd been dating. And what about his date he had recently with me?? He must have been dating her when we'd gotten naked on that conference center rug!

He started trying to explain why he'd asked her to marry him instead of me, but all I could see was his mouth moving while I felt my heart explode. I felt myself rise from the couch and head for the door as if I was watching someone else in slow motion. I opened it and told him, "Get the hell out! Get out, get out, and get the hell out!" It was all I could say, and it was all reaction. I couldn't actually think anything at all. Thankfully, Will didn't say a word and got out. I slammed the door and ran into the kitchen. I opened the first bottle of Budweiser and tilted my head back and let in flow into my system. I couldn't, can't, won't, this isn't real, deny, deny, deny. It wouldn't go away.

The second bottle followed quickly, then the third, while my mind replayed protests one after another. The more my mind swirled, the more the tears flowed and the more beer I guzzled until the fourth bottle chased the third.

Josaphine's Lessons

By the time I reached for the fifth bottle of beer, my roommates decided to come home early to satisfy their curiosity instead of going to the movies. They were suitably confused to see me sitting on the kitchen floor, crying like a banshee, surrounded by empty beer bottles, no man in sight. I'm sure I garbled an explanation that I had been thrown over for a nobody, and the only sound I was able to hear was, "I am going to marry someone else."

"That's not the worst!" I shouted, "No, no....The worst is he said he still wants to be my friend!" I got a lungful of air and shouted, "I wanted to be his wife! I was going to be his wife!" My roommates felt my pain, handing me the sixth bottle of beer, but safely removing the Jack Daniels, leaving my ass on the floor, because the battle to get me upstairs to bed would be a disaster.

Lesson learned– There's a reason it should go, "date first, fall in love together, then consummate." If you work with him, establish a solid friendship with the man of your dreams, so you know you can still be friends after a sexual encounter. Without it, you may discover that a couple of roommates, a hard kitchen floor, and a six pack of Budweiser, offer very little comfort with which to handle the unexpected surprises.

20

JACK – THE REPRIEVE

The name "Jack" will always hold special meaning for me as a wonderful name for a delightful black man. After my work encounter with another black man, I was granted a reprieve. Thinking of Jack, I immediately recalled his beautiful speaking voice and his quite prominent head.

He was my roommate's friend and associate, working with her at a downtown bank. When she set up a date for us, he came to our town house with flowers and chocolates. I couldn't believe my eyes! "Is he living in the wrong century?" I wondered. However, the sympathy in his eyes told me that my roommate had filled him in about what I was recovering from. Even as I smiled and accepted his gifts, I was thinking about how I would have to strangle her the moment I saw her for manipulating this poor guy.

Dinner was excellent and getting to know him felt entirely comfortable. He took me to a crab restaurant on the waterfront and we talked and talked the night away. He was cautious but firm as he held my hand when we walked along the harbor after dinner.

I couldn't have asked for a nicer man, but at first I couldn't help but think that perhaps he wasn't my type, and it might take some time and dating to find out for sure. We saw each other two to three nights a week over the following months, and after a while, I decided maybe my first assessment of Jack had been wrong. He showed nothing but kindness and was lovable all the time. In his quiet company my heart was certainly healing.

One day I got the sudden, bright idea that I would go over to Jack's apartment and surprise him. Sometimes that's not a good idea, I knew, but I was focused on a good outcome. When I got to his apartment, I saw his car and knew he was home. A sharp looking woman answered his door. She asked me in and offered me a seat. I knew Jack had a roommate and thought perhaps she was the roommate's girlfriend. She knocked on Jack's door and told him he had company. I hadn't met his roommate, so I kept expecting him to come in, any minute now. The woman looked me over again, smiled and went into the kitchen to stir some food that was on the stove. As she cooked, she asked if I wanted something to drink. I couldn't help noticing how familiar she was with the place and thought she must have been dating Jack's roommate for some time.

She brought me some soda and left it on the table, finding a coaster on the way, which seemed another too-familiar-with-the-place sign. Jack came out of his room yawning and froze, his mouth still open momentarily, when he saw me sitting in the living room, drink in hand. I went to him and he opened his arms to greet me, a gesture that somehow felt like he was greeting a sister. I hugged him tighter and whispered in his ear, "Who's the woman in the kitchen?" He didn't say anything for a moment, but then faced me and said she was his roommate. This was the roommate he'd told me about; she simply had a man's name. I wasn't shocked, just thankful he wasn't her boyfriend.

He came and sat down with me and asked why I came by. I couldn't think of a good enough excuse, so I asked if we could go in his room. He took me by the hand and led me to his bedroom. His room was rather large and a bit messy, with his artwork scattered around and every corner full of something. His bed was large and covered with laundry. He only had on jeans and a T-shirt and went into his closet. I followed.

His closet was pretty large and I commented about its size. I thought you could make love in this closet and no one would hear you. I didn't even realize I'd said that out loud! Jack looked at me and said, "What did you say?" In for a little, in all the way, I thought, so I took a deep breath and softly repeated those words. He grabbed me by my clothes and teasingly said, "You wouldn't! You're teasing!"

Oh, why did he have to set that challenge? It was like flipping a switch in me. I began taking my clothes off fast, moving before he could realize that I was not kidding. I got half disrobed and jumped on him. He fell back into a pile of shoes and dirty clothes, and I didn't care. Maybe it was the smell of testosterone all over the closet, but I was on autopilot. Somehow, I had shut the closet door with the closet light on, which was plenty to see what we were doing. Any thought of planning, judging, and more extended dating was gone. We came together so fiercely that clothes fell off the rack covering us like a blanket. We hardly noticed. There was no time for foreplay.

He felt around for my entrance with the head of his johnson and pushed into my wetness. I gasped for air and the smells in the closet plus his body against me, all came together as he drove into me. We gyrated, humped and ground together, gasping and grabbing for more. He stayed with me rhythm for rhythm for about ten minutes before we were done. As we came down from the rush, we rearranged ourselves and left the closet. I said goodbye to his roommate as though nothing had happened, pleasant as you please, and left the apartment happy I'd followed my instincts.

The next month we went to a dance that was held in a hotel room with a terrace that extended out to a picnic area. We were dancing on the terrace when he motioned for us to go over to a picnic table. He picked me up and sat me on the end of the table, pushing my sexy black dress up a little to arrange himself between my legs. We had become comfortable with intimacy quickly since our episode in his closet.

He was a hungry man when it came to sex, and loved different positions and little fun adventures. I wanted to make love right there and then on the picnic table, but he thought that we would get caught. Of course, my mind and body were vibrating for him to enter me. I opened my legs wider and said in my most seductive voice, "But, baby, I'm not wearing any panties under my sexy little dress." His grin told me the invite was going to happen!

He moved much closer into my grip and called me a very naughty girl, as he unzipped his pants and thrust deep inside me, pulling my legs around his waist. In the background we could see the small crowd dancing to another slow tune. I could feel my climax coming quickly and he sensed it, covering my mouth because he knew I was a screamer. He drove deeper and deeper into me as my bottom scratched against the rough surface of the picnic table. I didn't care, but I knew I'd be bruised and scratched up the next day. His hunger took over completely, and his passion pushed me with him over the edge and past the pain. He grabbed my ass and plunged in as far as he could go, and we climaxed together while we arched back and looked up at the stars.

Lesson learned– Be adventurous and challenging when you want to make love. It will please your lover and fulfill their appetite, and it will be as exhilarating as it is odd or dangerous. Places that seem impossible at first glance might suit just fine, if you give it a chance. Also, it is naturally essential not to wear panties when you are exploring for that opportunity.

21

CHARLES – WHEN NO IS NOT ENOUGH

The time was at last ripe for me to move to a less depressing place. I had the money and a good job. I was totally over living in an old, run down row house, in a town I didn't really care for. My roommates agreed to move up a notch, telling me it was long overdue. One roommate was not enthused about the idea and wanted to stay, but for the most part, when I brought it up one night, everyone else was on board.

I decided to hire a realtor to help me look for a new place, perhaps a refurbished row house. I put out the word and soon got a call back from a realtor named Charles. He sounded nice and had properties to present with a lease option to buy. That caught my interest, and we set an appointment to meet at a restaurant downtown after work.

When we met face to face, I thought he looked a little on the short side and a bit like my past, older boyfriend. The combination actually added up to my being attracted to him right away. He had a mustache, which was really quite attractive, and a monster smile, but somehow he had unemotional eyes. Someone must have hurt him, I thought, and somehow it didn't feel like he was healed.

We got to know each other a bit over dinner and it felt easy, like we were old friends, just getting reacquainted. He was all smiles and a good listener, making me comfortable. He poured on more charm and then asked, "Do you want to see my refurbished row house? It's not far from the East End." It jarred me somehow, and it set off red flags in my head, that little voice in the back of my mind, telling me I should just let him go. But, I was comfortable with him through some great conversations, a fabulous dinner, and a bottle of great wine that I skipped over those warning bells.

We left the restaurant and took his car into the East End. He parked in the back of a row house that looked absolutely new from the outside. The windows all had ornate bars on them, and the door was an iron gate. My warning lights started flying around in my brain like a tornado, but I still didn't do anything about it. We'd gotten along so well to that point that I deliberately turned off the "Josaphine Early Warning System," and was willing to see what lay ahead. He opened the door for me, which I thought was very gentlemanly. But when I stepped inside, something clicked—literally, I heard the noise as he slid home the dead bolt in the iron gate door, and then another distinct clack as he locked the house door as well. I saw they were both keyed dead bolts and I watched him pocket the key. My heart sped up and I admitted to myself that maybe the warning voices in my head were there for a reason, but I decided to play it cool and walked on into the living room. Maybe he was just being careful.

Furniture was sparse, with a small color TV against one wall, a couch, and love seat against the other. No pictures or mirrors. He asked if I wanted something to drink and, preoccupied, I said no. But I did allow him to show me around.

The hallway from the back door led to a loft opening and stairs off to my right. I hadn't noticed entrances and pathways at first glance, but as he walked me through the place, I started making note of the layout. He then showed me upstairs to an office, converted from a third bedroom, then the newly remodeled bathrooms and the loft windows with skylights above. It was a nice tour, but I was uncomfortable and thinking about the danger I might be in, looking for ways out. No way to get out from upstairs; downstairs windows all barred across; doors dead bolted. Not good, not good, not good. He showed me the master bedroom last and proudly proclaimed that this was where he did his best work.

He was getting so off the track that I wanted to throw up. The way things were playing, it felt like I was in some cheap horror movie getting set up for the murder scene. I tried to keep it together and did my best to stay calm and pleasant. He invited me to sit down on the bed, cool as you please, telling me we should make out. He had no apparent conception that his coming on to me wasn't really working; so, I played into that. I figured a little necking and I would get him to go back downstairs with me, giving me a chance to unlock the door and bolt.

But I was stumbling through the scene as well. I knew that his scheme was soooo off base, and with every moment, the evening grew ever more stilted. I couldn't come up with a way to break out of it! Charles, clueless, kept storming ahead with whatever plan he had cooked up. We were on his timetable, playing through his script. In what I'm sure to him was a "Mr. Cool" play, he asked me to take off my pants so he could really show me how to enjoy his kissing. It was dreadful to hear, nothing short of awful and repugnant. It just sent me over the edge, and I started to freak out inside my head.

I didn't want to have his hands on me, much less his tongue, and he was glibly ready to kiss me there....Well, come hell or high water, none of this plan was going to happen. I got up from the bed and headed to the bathroom. He smiled and asked if I was going to freshen up for him. I nodded and scooted out, trying to breathe. Closing the door, I sat on the toilet and thought frantically; nearly panicked. I could try to call someone. I'd seen a phone in the kitchen, but that meant getting back downstairs. He came to the bathroom door and asked if everything was okay. In that moment, the whole idea of planning my escape vanished. I swallowed my fears, stood and opened the door, ready to act, just not knowing exactly what to do—only to find the insensitive moron standing in front of me stark naked! Action came without awareness, without thought.

I flew past him and ran down the stairs and Charles followed after me, laughing hideously. "Oh, you want to play games!" he cackled madly. Every strange line out of his mouth lodged in my mind and seared into me word for word. "You overgrown teaser!" he yelled. There is no way he can be serious, I thought. He simply has to know I want out; I couldn't fathom him touching me again.

I ran into the kitchen and looked at the counter, but the phone wasn't there. Where was it...? I heard his thumping steps going into the living room, and then heard a cord snap as the phone was ripped from the wall. I knew I was the next target, nothing left to slow him down. I saw him heading towards me, and I desperately looked for anything to inflict pain, keeping him at bay—anything. The drawers were mostly empty; no flatware. He made it to the kitchen. Coming through the door, he threw the phone straight at me and said, "Go ahead and make your call."

I screamed for him to let me out, and he had the gall to say, "Over my dead body." He hardly raised his voice, but it punched coldly into me, as he told me I was going to give him what I had been flaunting at him all night.

Yes, earlier I had flirted with him, but I'd thought it was all in fun—normal. This naked moron was off the chain, and it was clear that he wanted me badly enough that he was willing to do anything, rape me even, to get what he wanted. He rushed me, hands held wide, calling me foul names as he came towards me. I already made up my mind about one thing: he was not going to touch me without paying a steep price. I swung and punched him in the face, catching him solidly. It didn't slow him much in his pumped up state, and he dodged the next swing. He closed in on me and tried to kiss me, ripping off my sweater at the same time.

It was time to get serious and make this end—it had to. I scratched his face and pulled at his hair, making a nasty girl fight out of it. He was going to feel it and he was going to bleed. He grabbed my face in his hands trying to kiss me again. I escalated things, got set and kicked him straight in the balls, hard, which was finally a message he would receive with some meaning!

He yelled and hunched over holding onto his precious jewels. It was all he could do to crawl away up the stairs, cursing me as he went. At last, I had bought some time. I heard him in the bedroom moving around. I didn't know what he was doing, but knew it would be nothing good for me. Time to depart...if I could get out.

First, I tried the back door, attempting to shake it open for all I was worth. I knew time was short, but it didn't budge. He called my name, screaming like I was in the next county. He appeared at the balcony, still naked, and now holding a gun, pointing it straight at me. He took a shot and it hit the wall right next to me.

I felt odd as though I might faint, but wide-eyed scared at the same time. Cornered with nowhere to run, I froze. He told me with a certain and serious tone in his voice that the next one would be in the middle of my forehead. I had to make a deal and give him whatever he wanted. If he wanted sex, I was ready to give it up, too, in exchange for more time on planet Earth. He was entirely high on whatever brain chemistry was happening to him; hardly in control. He grabbed his johnson and was shaking it at me, masturbating himself right there on the balcony, with his face making all sorts of contortions. I couldn't tell if he was going to rape me, shoot me or shoot off — or all three. I was a petrified spectator. He had definitely lost his damn mind.

I distantly heard my voice saying, "Okay, I'll let you screw me. On one condition. Afterward, I get to leave from here." I didn't let it get quiet either; I kept talking it up, stumbling around and trying to make the deal work. I'd give him my pants and go upstairs to wait, and he was to come down, unlock the door and put my pants next to the door. When he was finished with me, I would leave and never come back. I was probably babbling, but anything that worked and got him to not pull the trigger was a good plan. He laughed weirdly and said, "You know you're not in a position to make deals, sweetheart, but I want you. Ah, I want you so badly." As he talked, he came down the stairs, gun targeted on me the whole time, waving his member about like a limp, dish towel. He unlocked the door, leaving the key in the lock. I kept my eyes focused on him as I removed my pants.

No—he wanted the panties gone, too. I took them off and laid them on top of my pants. He pointed for me to go upstairs and followed, feeling my tight bottom.

Once in the bedroom he became another person. He mumbled endearments to me and tried to caress me gently, all the while holding the gun, bleeding a little from the scratches I'd left across his cheek and neck. He pulled me on the bed and laid me down, but he'd gone really soft. The next minutes were a frustrating agony for us both as he tried to get hard again. It didn't work; nothing worked, no matter what he did. His failure was my perfect rescue—everything about the night had changed again. He realized it at last and finally lowered the gun.

As he let go of it, I started to feel like I would get through the ordeal, and took a relieved exhale. Adding one more layer of crazy to an already crazy night, Charles asked if he could pick me up the next day so we could continue. For a second I couldn't believe I'd heard him right, but I remember thinking, "Well, that's not any stranger than what's been going on since we got here...!"

Flabbergasted, I wasn't about to turn away a gift horse that could get me out of here. I said, "Yeah, sure thing," as sincerely as I could manage, got up and started edging my way to the stairs. He followed, putting on his clothes. All I could think of was to get down stairs, get pants, put on pants, open door, go.... Hell, I think I was probably willing to skip the pants if it would get me out the door!

As I put my clothes back on at the door, Charles softly asked me if he could take me home. He wouldn't look at me and stared at the floor, away towards the wall. I could hardly believe it, but I heard myself say yes, please. Could he be feeling sorry for what he had done?

I began to think back to earlier that night when he was so incredibly nice and easy to get along with. I had to count on being with that earlier, nicer guy now, which is thankfully just how it turned out. He took me home in complete silence, even stopping along the way so I could run into a store and pick up a few things for work the next day. If I had called the cops from the store, I think he would've been sitting there in the car waiting, docile as could be. He'd been Dr. Jekyll, then Mr. Hyde; and on the way home, the kindly, sane gentleman was back in charge.

When I got home, my roommate was waiting up for me to hear about the new places. She immediately sensed something was wrong, and I started to cry as soon as I could grab her. I hated myself for what I let happen, and she held and comforted me. She led me inside and nudged me in the direction of a hot relaxing bath. She stayed with me constantly as I lowered myself into the water, and recalled for her the whole night. She was my lifesaver.

We both had tears flowing down our faces on and off for hours. Finally, she asked what I was going to do about it. Having had some time to gather my wits, all I said was that I had it figured out; that I had a plan. I told her that I will make a call in the morning. I said, "Let me see what develops, and I'll tell you the rest when I get home from work."

The next morning at work, I made a call to my one of my brothers. I told him everything. We went over and over the incident, hashing it out, and I could hear that he was a wreck over it. He would never wish harm on me from anyone. I gave him all the information I had on Charles.

Daily routine soon took over, and I was working through lunch when the switchboard brought in Charles's call. When I had him on the line, I stopped him from talking and quietly whispered that it was over, that I would hurt him until he screamed for mercy if he ever called, or came near me again. By itself, that probably wouldn't have held him back, lunatic that he was. But I also told him to expect a call, not from the police, but from my older brother. My brother the mortician! My older, crazy brother, the mortician, who enjoyed playing with dead people. I waited a second—no response. Feeling successful, I hung up, confident that the problem was going to be buried.

I never heard from my does-not-take-*No*-for-an-answer man again.

Lesson learned– When it's time to kick a guy's ass, give it everything you have and deliver it where it counts. If that fails and death is a possibility, do whatever you have to; anything in order to stay on Earth. If you have a moron on your case, call in a mortician who speaks "crazy," and let him explain the rules of revenge on your behalf.

22

JASON – MY FRIEND'S BROTHER

I knew that my best friend from school was getting married several states away, but I hadn't figured out how to get there. The date was nearly upon me. She was marrying a man who would be taking her away to England, making it a *must* to attend her wedding. We talked again closer to the date, and she promised me a bus ticket to Ohio. Also, she would find me a ride back to Washington, D.C. I agreed and started making travel arrangements.

The wedding was private, lovely, and the reception was a lot of fun. There were lots of people, including all her thirteen brothers and sisters with their families. It was a crowded affair with lots of dancing and drinking—definitely my kind of party!

Sometime during the fun, my friend's sister said that one of her brothers lived close to my home, and would be taking me back to D.C. in the morning. After my friend threw her bouquet, the happy couple was on their way to a blissful honeymoon. The party went on for a while and wound down well after dark. I had way too much fun and alcohol, too!

I slept in the room where my friend had been staying before the wedding, and it looked like she had been in a rush to leave. Her dress was hanging by a thread on the closet door, and there was a pile of clothing on the floor that I practically stumbled over. It was early when

I rose from my stupor and headed for the bathroom, watching where I stepped. I knocked on the door as I switched from one foot to the other doing the "pee pee dance." No one said anything, so I pushed the door open and looked for the toilet, only to find a tall, lanky man staring at himself in the mirror. I said I was so sorry, and he said for me to come in.

I was a bit surprised, but he said that this was his sister's house and his name was Jason. I introduced myself at the door and turned around to go back to the bedroom, shouting to please knock on the door when he was finished. I jumped on the bed and threw the covers over my face, embarrassed. A few minutes later he knocked on the door and walked in, and I could smell his scent invading the room—fresh Dove soap and Lagerfeld after shave. I was intoxicated immediately. Jason said he'd be taking me home and could I be ready in a half hour. I said, sure, with my head barely peeking from under the covers. He chuckled at me hiding, and said he was going to finish getting ready and to meet him in the foyer.

I don't know why I was scared. I agreed to catch a ride with him sight unseen, and it had seemed fine at the time. He was her brother, after all. My friend spoke very little of him, and I just felt a bit apprehensive. I had to be to work the next day, and D.C. was a ten hour drive away. That made my mind up for me, so I jumped out of bed, ran to the bathroom and quickly cleaned up.

Jason took my bags from me and put them in the car as I said goodbye to the rest of the family. Then, he came in and said goodbye to his family. His older sister shouted at him to behave and shook her finger, admonishing him to drive the speed limit. That made more sense when I saw a black-on-black, hot little Porsche in the driveway. "Oh, boy," I thought, "the trip is getting more and more interesting!"

Jason helped me into the passenger side and whispered, "So, are you scared?" I boldly said, "NO!" He laughed and said, "Well, you should be!" As he got into the driver side, I started to panic just a little. If he straight up tells me to be scared, maybe I should be, I thought!

"Perhaps I can take the train," I said as he got in. As he fastened his seat belt, he smiled and said, "Captain Jason at your service. Next stop, D.C. and your front door." I laughed nervously, and said that I didn't envision him making many stops along the way in this little rocket ship! I didn't need to worry about the ride because I really enjoyed the trip. Over a solid ten hours, we talked about everything from A to Z. By the time we got to D.C., I felt like I had known him all my life.

We pulled into my driveway, and acting the gentleman, he brought my baggage inside. He chatted about the next stage of his drive, which was five or six more hours to his home in North Carolina. I asked if he was tired and he said no, but when he yawned, it was an obvious fact. He'd driven the whole way, and I knew he needed a break. I asked him to lie down for a few hours and leave later. I nearly had to twist his arm and all but shoved him up to my bed for a nap. I wasn't afraid he would do anything to harm me, but he laughed, telling me to be scared again... and maybe I should have listened this time!

Jason slept soundly for a few hours, and I drifted off to sleep after he did. I watched him sleep and thought how very sexy he was; although, I didn't think he was really my type of man because I liked them bigger. He wasn't skinny, per se, just a small statured fellow. As I dozed, I dreamed that Jason was touching me on my back and shoulders. In my dream, I felt his hands travel down my length and rub my thighs. I could even feel him moving closer and rubbing up against me, which is what made me wake up. When I opened my eyes, I could immediately see what was going on in my mirror. Jason really was leaning over me and rubbing himself against my backside! He must have been playing with me for a while as I'd been dreaming, too, because I could feel my clothes completely in disarray.

What the hell! I had to admit the dream had been a happy one. I had been thinking maybe I did want to screw his brains out—but a girl likes to be asked! Well, maybe this was him asking.... I opened my mouth to say something, but he quickly put his tongue in my mouth and started to kiss me with a fully aroused passion. No words needed after all! I felt fairly aroused myself when I woke up, and it seemed to be getting better—downright hot and shameful, in fact! This was my friend's brother, for heaven's sake....

He lifted my body against the head board and slid up behind me. He pulled my gown up over my waist and told me to hold on as he slightly bent over me and thrust his large erection inside me. Where the hell did that come from? I was ready enough to receive it, however, and it felt damn good, stretching me as he entered. Where was he hiding that heaven? Jason, the small one, certainly didn't feel small in the johnson department! He was strong and filling and I gasped thinking how much of him was inside me. He began a rhythm that was stimulating and pulsating as I moaned and groaned to his moves, and I used my grip on the bed to push back onto him. After a little while he increased the speed, until we both shouted in ecstasy as he poured his seed deep inside me. I worked up a sweat as though I'd just run a marathon, and then I collapsed. He released himself from me and turned me around to kiss me more into oblivion. I felt sated beyond measure and in a happy fog.

He asked to freshen up, and I pointed in the direction of the bathroom. He left me for a short time, showered and came back fully dressed and ready to leave. He kissed me goodbye and left without me even walking him to the door.

Lesson learned– Don't ride in a hot sports car thinking it's not foreplay. If you invite a tired man into your bed, they may rest, but soon after they will be ready to take you for a different kind of exotic drive. Just hold on and enjoy both rides!

23

KENNY – I'M CLUELESS

I dated Kenny for a while, and the time came when he wanted me to visit his apartment. I was a little apprehensive, since my last few decisions hadn't been for the best, but I really liked this guy. He was tall and slender with well-defined muscles to hold it all together. He was strong and, of course, he'd passed my main test of being an absolutely fabulous kisser.

On the night in question, we first went to dinner at an oyster bar on the harbor where I tried raw oysters for the first time. I was amazed how those babies just slid down my throat. A chaser of vodka with a lemon twist was another new experience for me. With Kenny, it was about trying new things. I loved that part of our relationship and looked forward to what he would dream up next. It was, however, this same "always trying new things" aspect of Kenny that made me ask myself later, "Why didn't I get the first clue?"

As the oysters kept coming, so did the vodka shots and before long, I was feeling pretty tipsy. I asked Kenny to get us a cab. By then I was ready, willing and able and added, "To your apartment!" We laughed and joked around in the cab, but then he started talking lewdly. He spilled some amazingly raunchy things in my ear; things that made my eyes get pretty big around. He had me gasping for air, but I ended up just laughing them off as "titillating chatter." I should have been sitting up and saying, "Wait a minute, there, mister," but still, I didn't get the second clue.

His apartment was a small studio; first, you enter a living room area that has a kitchenette and bathroom off to the left. Then, straight back was a queen-sized bed and dresser. Kenny went to the bathroom first and when he came out, I was laying on the bed on my back with my feet on the floor. I knew he wanted me and I wasn't opposed to a little fun, but I could tell something was different about him when he came out of the bathroom. Seriousness had replaced his relaxed demeanor and any perception of being loosened up or tipsy from our drinking vanished. He had a gleam of real mischief in his eyes, which in hindsight, was clue number three passing quickly by.

Something about all these clues must have been working away in my subconscious. As I freshened up in the bathroom, washed my face and stared in the mirror, I wondered if I could magically make myself reappear back at my apartment. I wanted to put off this dreadful rendezvous. Regrettably, my rescue-me guard was off for the night, and I was going to have to get through it. After all, I told myself, I'd gone out that night ready for some hanky-panky right from the start.

When I came out the bathroom, he was laying on the bed fully dressed. I thanked all kinds of folks and God as I lay down next to him. He was gentle when he kissed me and started to massage my back. He must have felt the nervous tension in me and pulled me closer to him for more warm-up kissing. He really was a great kisser and his tongue was making gentle strokes in my mouth, leading me to the feeling that this might be what it would be like to make love to him.

He started to undress me and I sat up to let him take all my clothes off. He put me under the covers and then turned out the lights. He joined me under the sheets but, oddly, he kept his shirt and pants on. I figured maybe he wanted me to undress him the rest of the way, but he pulled me close, stopping me. The feel of his clothing against my naked body was kind of stimulating so I went with it. We began kissing again while he rubbed me all over. I was so totally into what he was doing that I started scolding myself for doubting his intentions. The oddity of his clothes, the fourth clue, thus sailed right over my head.

He got out of the bed and asked me to turn around. "He must want to take me from behind," I thought. I turned over and then I heard the softest of clicks and a vibrating hum. I jerked around so fast that I almost flew off the bed. Clue number five wasn't hard to imagine, and I shouted, "What the hell is going on?" He smiled and said, "Say hello to my not-so-little friend!"

The vibrator he was holding was long and pink and I asked him, "So, just where are you intending to introduce your friend to me?" Sarcasm always has seemed a good ice breaker as my first line of defense. He replied, "In your behind! Isn't that where you like it?" We were well past hints and clues! "Oh, shit, I have got to turn this butt buster around," I thought. I was sure I could put a stop to it when I said, "Hell no, I don't think so, freak! How about I stick that up your ass?" Given that my angry tone of voice wasn't inviting, he went past my last line of defense when he didn't get my "clue." Instead, he smiled even bigger and said, "That would be perfectly awesome!"

Lesson learned– When you're dating "nice guys" who want to "try new things" all the time, get around to talking about their sexual preferences well in advance! Real clues about what you're in for may come slowly at first, and then come at you too damned fast to assimilate in the heat of the moment.

24

ROGER – THE SHY ONE

When I moved to the Boston area, I left a lot of memories, friends, and furniture back in Baltimore. I planned to return to Baltimore and get my things after I was settled with a job and a place to live. It took six months to finally decide it was time to rent a truck and head back for my belongings. I missed my furniture, antiques and books. I made arrangements with my former roommates, and they set up moving people to help load my things into the truck.

I arrived late on a Saturday afternoon, and the moving folks were already waiting. They packed my belongings into the truck leaving me free to rest. I planned to leave early Sunday morning, which had seemed like a safe plan. I foresaw no hiccups with the whole plan, but something can always throw a monkey wrench in the works. This time the wrench was named Roger, and he arrived on the scene late in the day.

Roger was a well-built, stocky sort of fellow, a bit on the shy side. Without saying much, he jumped right in, lifting furniture and boxes without the least strain. He was full of breathe going up and down the stairs, and I watched him the whole time as he bent over and flexed his muscles for me all evening. He was a sweaty sight to behold, and I'm not sure to this day if he knew what an impression he was making. As I watched him sweating away, it wasn't a stretch for me to start plotting and planning how to show him just what certain muscles could do for a woman.

I knew he had a crush on me for at least a year, but all my friends told me to leave the poor guy alone. He must have known he was putting himself in the line of fire with me. Why else would he have been there? That was fine by me, and I planned to quench the fire as soon as the last item was loaded on the truck.

As the night grew late and things wound down, I brought pizza and beer and we all settled down to eat and relax. It was a pleasant affair with light banter, but I was plotting my move on Roger. We all laughed and sweated, and then we laughed some more, as we realized how horrible we smelled from running up and down the stairs all evening. Later, the roommates went to bed leaving me sitting with Roger in the living room on a fur rug in a corner. Since my furniture was gone, the place was pretty barren, and until my former roommates got new furniture, there wasn't anything to sit on. Somehow, it made things more intimate; more relaxed.

Roger was leaning against the wall near the open window looking down to the street. I scooted up close to him and asked if he had to go home. He said he might stay a little longer, and then he looked at me. I focused on his puppy dog, brown eyes and could see in his face that he'd been longing to kiss me for so long. It was very quiet in the apartment as I got up and closed the door. We were alone, and I heard Roger's heavy breathing for the first time that evening. I could tell he was nervous to be alone with me. I didn't blame him, because he was definitely going to be panting in a few minutes.

I had a dress on, was clean and fresh, because I'd taken a quick shower while folks ate. I moved my infamous plans forward, too, and was naked underneath, moving in for the pleasure I knew was waiting. I walked back over to Roger, leaned over him and kissed him full on the lips. I pushed my tongue into his mouth, grabbed his face and kissed him with everything I had to give. We both moaned from the pleasure of it, and I embraced him fully, sitting straight down on his lap. He sat up straighter, which pressed his bulging pants into me. I had his undivided attention and could feel his erection pressing into my moistness. I was going to stain his pants if I didn't do something, so I lifted up without stopping the kiss and unzipped his pants.

He grabbed my wrist and said into my mouth, "We can't!" His body said otherwise. I removed his hand from my wrist and gently pulled his erection out of his pants, careful not to hurt him against the zipper. He just stared at me and then gave himself over to my ministrations. I lifted up and placed his hardness at the opening of my core and impaled myself on him. He met me with surging force, and his strong response pushed us into a sex-hazed zone I totally expected. I let the dance take over and we found a rhythm. It was so hot and urgent while our clothes stayed on, ignoring them as we stayed in the groove. We climaxed together while kissing demandingly into each other's moans and groans. As we recovered, the room became still and silent again. Roger never said another word, looking at me with that sweet puppy dog expression.

I lifted myself from him and went to the bathroom to cleanse myself. I thought what a fiend I was to take advantage of him and his crush, but it didn't feel wrong. I smiled as I realized just how good he felt and how right it was to me. I brought him a wash cloth and gently washed his member. I put it back in his pants and lay down on the floor next to him. He didn't say anything, holding me close. Before I knew it, I was asleep, and then it was morning.

I woke to a stiffness that was unbelievable, but even as I was wiping the sleep from my eyes, I had a satisfied smile. As I woke up, I planned to make the most of it and ask Roger to visit me in Boston. But, as I looked around, I noticed he was gone. I never saw him again.

Lesson learned– When you have a shy man, for his sake, you might want to listen to your friends when they tell you to leave him alone. I'm sure that shy, quiet Roger was forever branded by my brazen desires.

25

JOE – THE PRIZE BULL

I was so thankful to be living in Boston that I often walked along the streets, looking into different stores and riding the trains and trolleys. I eventually got three female roommates, and we lived together in a nice, mostly black neighborhood. Our place was sandwiched between the North End and the East End neighborhoods.

Each neighborhood, we discovered, had its own bars; each in its own way defining the area and serving its own regulars. The four of us became regular customers at one such bar close to our home. After a few months of going there to dance and drink, several people knew us by name, and we became a part of the scene there. We started dating the neighborhood men, and we'd come to think of the club as our own. In particular, I had my eyes on The Prize Bull.

As I came in the door one night, Joe was already putting a drink on the counter for me. I smiled and asked how he knew what I wanted, and he said by the way I parked my car. He could somehow tell just from that, that I'd had a rough day. I smiled and corrected him to say it had been, in fact, a rough week.

I had gone to the shrimp market to get some fried shrimp and fries for one of my roommates, and I knew I smelled like shrimp and grease. I found my friends at a table and joined them as I thanked Joe for caring. He smiled and said he would dance with me later.

I hadn't noticed what Joe was wearing behind the bar, but an hour or so later and true to his word, he was looking for me on the dance floor. I watched him from the hallway near the restrooms and grinned, knowing he wouldn't see me staring. He was dressed in all black tight leather and God, I thought, he was some slick eye candy, like black licorice. His pants and jacket had no room to breathe as he guided his tall, massive form around the floor.

I took a little more time to admire him from the hall. His hair was cropped to a close fade on a very large head. I could see his expression from across the room, and he wore a tight grin that looked lethal, ready to deal with anybody that didn't move out of his way. I, on the other hand, knew I was his "target," so at last I stepped up to him and said, "You looking for me?" He smiled large and said, "Let's ride!" I went to the table and told my roommates bye, and they snickered and laughed to see me heading out with the infamous and imposing Joe.

He was hungry and took me to a greasy sub place that made the best steak and cheese subs in all of Massachusetts. I ate little, planning ahead and not knowing what was on Joe's mind; I'd learned early on that for me, greasy food and sex were not compatible. We didn't engage in subtle chit chat, and I asked if he wanted to go to my place since my roommates were still at the club. He grunted and got back in his sleek black-on-black convertible and headed for my apartment. I knew this wasn't the first time Joe had been to my place, so while he navigated, my mind was focused, wondering what the hell to do with this bull of a man once we got there.

He pulled up to my apartment and ran over to open my car door. Well, that was sweet. It's a good sign.... He opened all the doors as we ascended to the second floor apartment. He opened the French glass door to my apartment and allowed me to pass through. My dogs came bounding from the back of the apartment, happy that someone had at last come home to let them out. They bolted past me and Joe and went to the first floor doors to be let out. Joe even volunteered to take them up to the park, and I sighed with relief. I felt burned out from my week and not in the mood to play or walk them.

While Joe walked the dogs, I changed, freshened up and made drinks. I knew he drank beer, so I had one ready. He let the dogs back in and came to join me in the den. I sat on the couch with my feet curled under me and enjoyed watching him move about. He was like a grand bull in a China shop, but he didn't stumble about at all. He took the beer I offered and sat in the chair next to the couch. He was a man of few words and looked at me intensely as he downed his beer in a long gulp. He put the bottle down as he reached for me to come and sit on his lap.

I wasn't sure the chair would hold the both of us, but he took charge immediately and pulled me close. He placed one hand on my back to steady me, and the other went around my waist close to my breasts. I didn't want to mess up his leather pants, but he told me to be still. He kissed me gently at first, and I could fill his need rising below me. I had on a New England Patriots' football shirt that came just below my knees, and nothing else.

I kissed him back and pushed deeper into his lap. He lifted the front of my shirt and placed his fingers at the juncture of my thighs. I took a deep breath as he slid a finger inside me. The room started to feel hot, and I could feel sweat growing on my face. He made love to me with his fingers until I screamed out an enormous orgasm against his hand. His lips never left my face and all I could do was hold on for dear life.

My prize bull had claimed me, and I felt his hardness enter me with jubilation. He'd lifted me and set me on his shaft hastily. He felt so damned good inside me. I couldn't wait to have this mountain of a man on top of me. He drove into me again and again, and we grew more and more forceful until we literally demolished the chair. We went crashing to the floor as it gave way from the friction and heat of our joining. We set the chair ablaze. Joe wasn't fazed at all and never stopped his intense desire, scooping me up and carrying me to the bedroom to continue. I was in complete bliss the whole time, and to this day, how his skintight leather clothes came off is still a secret.

Most of what I remember is how incredibly sated I was to be mounted by the prize bull of the neighborhood bar.

Lesson learned– Your "prize bull" in a China shop will eventually break something, but it won't be anything you can't fix or replace later! Hold on tight and enjoy the bouncy ride. If you can hold on longer than eight seconds, you will be awarded *thee* grand prize.

26

LARRY – THE MERCEDES OVERLOAD

One day in the club, a man named Larry was bragging about his new car. Well, he didn't have to tell anybody it was a Mercedes. The logos blazoned across his jogging suit, the jangling keychain and his monogrammed cap were signs enough. He was excited, to say the least. Any excuse to party is a good one, I figured. Why not cash in on the excitement? Maybe he'll buy me a drink.

Larry eventually made his way to our table and asked me to dance as a slow song was starting. My roommates chuckled, as once again, I was providing the amusement for the table. I smiled back, thinking they were just jealous; it wasn't them dancing with Mercedes Larry. He danced with me gently and pulled me close to sing the song in my ear. Oddly, his singing didn't put me off at all, as I realized he had a nice voice. As he came to a tricky spot in the song, I giggled wondering how he would handle it. He handled it by switching from singing to smooching. While I lifted my head to his face to see what he'd do with the song, he kissed me, giving me tongue right then and there on the floor.

My roommates hooted and howled like they were at a rodeo. I quickly broke the kiss and put my head back on his shoulder. It was dark, so no one could see me blushing. That kiss wasn't half bad, and Mr. Mercedes had passed my kissing requirement with flying colors!

He whispered in my ear that he wanted to take me for a ride, and I gladly accepted.

He took me for a drive across the city to an all-night diner for some breakfast. That was fine with me, as I liked breakfast anytime of the day. After I listened to him talk about his car through the entire meal, I was ready to go as soon as we finished our food. As we left the restaurant, he asked me to spend the night with him, and I agreed. I was willing to see if his apartment matched his ride, and if his bedroom moves matched his kissing, singing and dancing.

He pulled into the garage under a swank, high-rise complex, and my mouth fell open. Mercedes Larry lived large, it appeared, and I was duly impressed before we'd even gotten inside. He pulled into a parking space with an apartment number and came to open my door. After an elevator ride to a high numbered floor, we went into his apartment. The view was amazing. My mouth was still on the floor when he turned on the lights and asked if I liked his place.

It was a studio apartment and in one sweep, you could glance at the whole place like a big box. I immediately felt that enclosed feeling. What the heck was I to do? I no more wanted to sleep with him here, than with a horse in a barn. Stunned, I realized I didn't even see a bed. Mercedes Larry's prospects were definitely cooling down rapidly.

He went to the couch and took off the pillows. Oh, God! No—he is not going to pull out a sleeper sofa bed. But to my continued astonishment, he did, and to top it off, the fold-a-bed had a Mercedes comforter on it! I finally found the nerve to speak and said, "Larry, would you mind taking me home? I don't feel so good at the moment." He looked at me with displeasure and pouted. "But I wanted to have you here. We don't have to screw around or anything...." I kept insisting and soon enough, I got to the basic complaint as he said, "It's just, I don't have enough gas to take you home and come back again."

I looked through my purse and took out a twenty, and told him he should have mentioned to me his finances were low. I asked him to call me a cab and crept closer to the door. Almost as though it was on cue, his shoulders slumped and he started to cry. Tears were streaming down his face.

"Oh, hell no! Larry, what the hell is the matter?" I asked, completely put off.

He said no one had ever come to hang out at his place and he wanted to be friends with me. He said I was so beautiful and fun, not like other girls from the club who'd been mean to him, and took advantage of him. He was a sad sight from head to toe. I came away from the door and sat down on the edge of the bed. I told him to come to me, and he shuffled across the room like a little puppy. I took off my shoes and lay down on the uncomfortable bed, and Larry crawled next to me and put his head on my breasts. I slapped his hands from roving and dried the tears from his face with a tissue. No sex, no playing around, but I told him I would stay the night with him, and he could take me home in the morning.

He was so glad to have company sleeping over; I'm sure his mind never left the thought of getting some. He went into the bathroom and came out wearing pajamas covered with the Mercedes emblem and name from top to bottom. Oh, for heaven's sake! I thought—but out loud I said, "Nice PJs," as he hopped onto the pull-out bed next to me. It's a wonder the thing didn't collapse.

Truth really seemed stranger than fiction as he leaned over the side of the bed and pulled out a teddy bear with Mercedes pajamas on it. The night was so far gone, I could only smile and ask if he wanted me to tell him a bedtime story. He said only if it was about Mercedes, and I assured him it would be the best story about Mercedes cars he ever heard. I started making up anything I could as though I was babysitting a small boy, and he fell fast asleep after the first few minutes.

Lesson learned– Sometimes it isn't always about sex. Letting a man do his thing and not condemning him for it has a place in the scheme of things, too. It's fine that "boys will have their toys," and even though both the boy and the toy are man-sized, you may find that the man hasn't grown up at all. Be prepared; they might need a good bedtime story.

27

MIKE – THE MONKEY MAN

Sometimes, like it or not, your friends or roommates may comment negatively on your choice of a date. It's just roommate nature. Tonight, my roommates decided my date of the moment, Mike, should be named "Monkey Man." I didn't like this nickname, but I said nothing to them. I was not amused, but as rude as they were, in hindsight, they were right on the money.

I met Mike while walking my dogs in the park. He was not a very tall fellow and he walked sort of funny, but it was cold out and I thought he might have been chilly. He seemed nice, though, and he asked me out.

He was dark skinned and hairy, but he had a lot of teeth and they were really white. Oddly, he could actually roll his top lip back on itself to reveal his gums. The first time I thought I might kiss him, it didn't feel right. He didn't feel right in my arms either for some reason. Still, I thought he was a very nice man, not married with any children. Those men were getting hard to find, and I resolved to be appreciative.

One night we stayed up watching a movie at my place, and my roommates were out of sight in the kitchen. The rest of the house was dark, just some light spilling out dimly from my room. Mike asked if he could kiss me, and I decided to try it again. I loved kissing and perhaps he deserved another chance. Since we were lying on the couch, I thought it might feel somehow different. I was right. He was just the right height when lying side by side.

The kisses were going along splendidly, better than expected, when his hands started to roam. He started kissing his way to my breast and stomach. All I wanted to do was kiss, just that, so I asked, "What are you doing?" He said, "Let's take this to your room." I hesitated, but he jumped off the couch and pulled me to my feet. He was deceptively strong. As we stood, he kissed me again, this time throwing me literally off balance. It seemed he was always jumping up or standing on his toes, and in this case, he put us in an uncomfortable embrace.

I put it behind me and let him lead me to my room. As we entered, before I could warn or control him, he saw my waterbed and started rolling around on it like a kid with a new, fun toy. My waterbed was heated and had mirrors in the head board, so in a way it was a great "toy." It was heavenly to sleep in when you got in the right spot, but dangerously unsteady with one person moving around, let alone two. Mike kept moving and testing it out until I asked him to stop so I could get on the bed.

He settled down, peeling off his clothes and kneeling on the bed. Kneeling is definitely a no-no on this kind of bed! The water was pushed all to one side, which lifted me up. Then the momentum swung back and rolled me into him, knocking him completely off the bed. The recoil from him leaving threw me back the other way, and I hit the side of the bed. I slid down until I was squashed between the side board and the mattress. I thought the evening was turning into an escapade with a trampoline at the zoo. Mike's spirits, however, weren't dampened in the least. He said he thought the whole thing was great fun as he pulled me up from where I was trapped. As soon as I was back upright, he ran around to the other side and jumped on it again, like a kid on a fun ride. This time I wasn't on the bed, and I got to watch as Mike did some sort of strange, hopping dance on the waterbed. He couldn't stop watching himself in the mirrors.

Here was my date, dancing butt naked on my bed, with his johnson flinging around like a yoyo. I finally got exasperated and asked him to stop jumping around. My anger was only made worse when I realized at that moment, it was pretty easy to see why my roommates called him Monkey Man. To make matters more comical, he actually got into the role, beating his chest and making "oo, oo" sounds as he bounced about.

I might have recovered from this silliness and wacky behavior, but finally, the waterbed couldn't take anymore abuse. The next sounds I heard were the squishes of a wet monkey on a wet bed! Mike stopped jumping and looked down at the results of his pranks. His feet were wet and water was beginning to pool and spread. I shouted for Mike to get off and ran to the closet for my water mattress repair kit. Mike, seemingly clueless about how upset I was, continued to be amused. "For God's sake, Mike! Put something on and help me fix the bed!" I blurted. I scrambled to control the bleeding water. Still and forever clueless, he looked at me as if I had sprouted horns and said, "Why, I didn't break it!"

That little snide remark pushed me completely over the edge, and as he bent over to pick up his clothes, I kicked him square in his ass and stormed out of the room. He ran after me down the hall and into the kitchen. I stopped in the kitchen's doorway, hands on hips, and looked at my roommates as they sat playing cards. The look on my face and the soundtrack they must have been listening to, lit their faces with smirks at my expense. They looked at one another, looked back at me and said in unison, "We told you!"

Lesson learned– If you don't want to hear the "I told you so!" line, remember that Monkey Men and waterbeds are not a good mix. If things get wobbly in the kissing department, they will get wobbly everywhere else, too. Just let him go and wait for the next opportunity to come, keeping you and your waterbed safe from any monkey business!

28

LUCIUS – SALT AND PEPPER MAN

After my wet adventure with monkey man, I was back at the neighborhood club with my roommates. I saw a man so distinguished looking and handsome, I thought he was too exquisite for our little bar. But he seemed right at home, and looking our way, he spotted something he liked and made his way to our table. One of my roommates laid claim and told everyone at the table that he was hers. Since I had recently dated someone else from the club, she said it was only fair that it be her turn. I couldn't argue with her logic, but I did point out that I was the only single presently available to date.

"Hello ladies, I'm Lucius. I own the African boutique and gift shop a few doors down and would like to invite you to come in and browse around." At the mention of the boutique, I thought I recalled seeing him in that shop. Because he seemed so classy, I wouldn't necessarily have pegged him as the owner. I assessed him from head to toe and immediately liked what I saw.

He seemed at ease, wearing a decorative dashiki shirt over a turtle neck sweater, nice-fitting black jeans, and cowboy boots. He was tall and handsome, and the icing on the cake was his salt and pepper, short cropped hair, beard and mustache, neatly trimmed and very sexy. His eyes were intensely black and his skin was smooth as creamy mocha. I noticed that his hands were manicured as he shook our hands and made pleasantries. After a bit, he moved on to the next table.

The next day, I was headed to the bar to meet my friends and roommates, when I happened to pass his store. Remembering his invitation, I pulled my coat tighter against the cold and went in. He was closing up for the day and didn't see me right away. When he noticed me, he turned around and blinked as though he was surprised. I said, "Hi, I'm here to take you up on your offer to browse." I headed for the counter where he was standing to look at the jewelry, and he said he was getting ready to close, but to take my time.

I commented on a few pieces I thought were nice and bought a pair of silver hooped earrings. He thanked me and then asked me to join him for a drink next door. I hadn't expected it, but I managed to stutter my agreement, all the while thinking, "A thousand times, yes!"

We went to the bar and had happy hour cocktails, his treat. I couldn't stay long and left after an hour, but not before inviting him to come to lunch at a house where I worked in the richer section of town. I gave him the address and phone number there and went home, looking forward to a big day to come.

Lucius joined me for lunch around 1:30 p.m. just as I finished an appointment with the staff. Everyone was leaving for the day, and I needed to finish some correspondence before we could go. Lucius asked if it would be possible to see the rest of the house. I was happy to show him around, and it gave me a chance to tell him about my position. I would be housesitting for a week, but the man of the house was still around until the next day.

As we went through the second floor of the house, the room that fascinated Lucius the most was the Jacuzzi bathroom. He was astonished at the size of the tub, which was quite inviting and large enough to hold four people. Smiling, I invited him to come back and join me in there later in the week. He grinned in a very sexy way for a response and confirmed his interest. We continued our tour into the attic, and he grabbed my behind and squeezed. I jumped up the stairs and told him not to be so naughty; but, I was lying.

In my head, I silently hoped he would be naughty all he wanted. He seemed to like the cramped space of the one-bedroom attic, if for no other reason than it forced us close. I told him that this is where I stayed when I took care of the place. The bed was small and cramped, but he sat down and pulled me into his arms. I was so wrapped up in wanting him by that point that I boldly told him that he could take me here, there, and anywhere it suited his fancy. I wanted him and wasn't subtle in the least! He kissed me so thoroughly that time seemed to stand still. He smelled so good; tasted so delicious. All my senses were heightened and drank in his sexy atmosphere. I pushed him back on the bed and straddled him.

He broke the kiss (oh, that man was a master kisser!) and whispered sweet nothings in my ear. Naughty nothings, too! As I was losing myself in the fantasy of the moment, I realized what I was seeing out the port window next to the bed. It was the man of the house pulling into the driveway. I thought for certain we were going to be caught in the act. Another few seconds, and I would not have been looking at anything outside! I broke off fast and told Lucius we had to go, though I knew it meant that his aroused bulge would have to wait. He said we were going to his place to finish what I'd started, with a bit of determination in his voice, and I didn't disagree!

We managed to slip out to his big "deuce and a quarter," an old type of a very large Buick. The front bench seat could fit three comfortably, but he pulled me close, saying he didn't want to lose the heat flaring between us. It was going to be at least a twenty minute ride to his place, even with the smooth traffic before rush hour. We were both impatient, anticipating what was coming. He came to a stop sign at the bottom of the hill near my job, just moments from our departure, and pulled me closer for another mind boggling kiss. I trembled under his intensity and nearly forgot where we were. He pulled my hand down on his erection and moaned. I knew this was going to be a throbbing but enjoyable ride!

I pulled away from the kiss and he started to say something, but he valiantly paid attention to driving and pulled into traffic. I was still holding his throbbing through his pants and caressing him gently. Even as he reacted and moaned excitedly, he was speeding onto the highway. I only had eyes for one thing, and within minutes I unzipped his pants to pull his member out so I could feel him in my hands.

As I massaged his hardness, he sighed and arched up into my hand, jamming his foot down in order to rise up, hitting the gas. As we sped up down the road, I brought my head down and took him fully into my mouth. He gasped as I kissed the tip of him. It must have been too much for him to handle, because he took the first available exit and stopped forcefully, taking a moment to regain control.

We were only half way to his place. As he continued to drive, I didn't stop. I was fully engrossed in my activity and enjoying it. Soon he was driving with both hands clenched on the wheel. After a minute, he seemed to gain a rhythm and more control. He positioned one hand on the back of my head and stroked it, so I would pull harder on his member until he finally exploded, screaming loudly. I had no idea where we were as the car turned quickly and came to an abrupt halt. We landed in his driveway.

As I sat up, I saw the smile on his face. He said, "Amazing! You drew on me all the way home. I was so into you that I was driving and looking around going, 'Hey, I got a lady kissing my johnson as I'm driving!' I couldn't stop grinning. I felt like I was on top of the world."

He pulled me into him and said he would gladly return the favor. I asked to go inside and he said no, to get in the back seat. We made love in that deuce and a quarter for the next hour, in his driveway. He not only returned the favor but stored more favors for another drive around the city. Coming up for air, I told him next time I get to drive and he gets to kiss, and that we would just have to figure out how we were going to accomplish that without going to jail!

Lesson learned– Be ready to prove your worth, because when the opportunity comes, you will need your ingenious kissing abilities ready to perform. After the final explosion, you can enjoy all the rewards afforded you. It also pays to know how to handle hard packages with delicacy while you're on the road. Happy driving!

29

ELVIS – AN AFRICAN PRINCE

One day, I was doing some errands for my employer and went into a specialty shop for an exotic item she wanted. On that side of Boston the area was very transient. People wandering Kenmore Square probably attended any number of colleges in the surrounding area.

I was in the store less than five minutes, when a man came up to me and said he liked my hair. His accent was interesting, and when I looked at him I said, "You aren't from here, are you?" He smiled with a mouth full of pearly whites and said, "No, I am from Africa. I am visiting the area for the summer. My name is Elvis."

My mouth dropped, I'm sure, as I said to him, "You're kidding, right? Your name's Elvis! Wow!" He said yes, he had been named after the King. I told him it had been nice to meet him and wished him a pleasant stay. I went back to my shopping but noticed he was following me around the store and watching me. I was getting a little agitated when he approached me again.

"I'm sorry for staring," he said, "but I would love to take you to dinner." I said, "No" as I was a little put off by his lurking. He seemed kind and genuinely interested when he smiled even more and said, "Well, I would like to get to know the lady underneath that fabulous, cropped hairstyle. Not many women can wear such a style!"

I thought he was way too flattering, but somehow I caved and instead of the planned "no, thank you," I found myself smiling back and saying, "Sure, why not."

He asked where we could meet, and I cautiously suggested someplace open where lots of people would be around, someplace really pricey. He didn't look like money would be an object, and he readily agreed on Trader Vic's for dinner at eight.

I arrived late to find my well-dressed, African gentleman looking about for me impatiently. He saw me walking towards the restaurant from the train and joined me, scolding me by way of greeting for not allowing him to pick me up at my door. Of course, I didn't want him to know where I lived, but I just smiled and made light of it. I was willing to give him a chance in this first date, to get to know each other and see what developed.

He found me more perplexing as the evening wore on, asking many questions about being a Black American and the culture I grew up in. When he finally asked what I did for a living, he wasn't familiar with the concept of housesitting, which made for a bit of a giggle. "Can the house not just be alone?" he asked in his thick, French-African accent, genuinely lost. I tried to explain, and then simply asked him to come by my office the next day. I would show him the house, and we would shop together for things I was looking for earlier that day. He gladly accepted, and after a friendly and enjoyable evening, we concluded our dinner. As I rose to leave, he insisted on giving me a ride home. It was getting very late, and I felt much more comfortable with him after our time together, so I accepted.

When the valet brought his car around—I nearly fainted. I had never seen a Lamborghini up close and personal. More amazing still, it was lime green! I just stared at it and my mouth just plain hung open. If there was ever a time to gawk, I thought, this was it! I realized I never asked Elvis what he did for a living.

When the doors rose in the air and the valet stepped out, I was still in a stupor. I remember thinking, "Am I really getting to ride in this sexy car? Hell yeah!!" Elvis helped me into the passenger side and

Josaphine's Lessons

strutted to the driver's side, tipped the valet and got in. "Where do you live, my love?" he asked in his thick accent. I gave him directions to my job. Since I was still housesitting, he would know how to get there for lunch tomorrow, plus I still wasn't ready to take him to my home.

He drove naturally and smoothly like he was used to being surrounded by such an excellent performing car. I was absorbed by the experience though, thrilled and excited to be in such an amazing, sexy machine. "Definitely a foreplay object!" I thought. But I'm not succumbing to its pull tonight. Hmmm—maybe tomorrow! I don't know if anyone saw me get out. I sure took my time and felt a little special as he dropped me off.

The next morning, I got an early call from Elvis saying he couldn't wait to see me again. I had some errands to run and he asked if he could take me. The decision wasn't tough! The thought of running around all morning in a Lamborghini enticed me!

He came to the house wearing jeans, sneakers and a V neck sweater instead of a shirt. He looked a lot better in his casual attire; more laid back and comfortable. He came in while I gathered my list of places to visit, then we quickly headed to the driveway. Parked in the drive was a mint condition, red convertible Dodge Stealth, top down. Once again, I opened my mouth and thought, "Holy shit! Who is this guy? What was this, his casual car?"

He opened my door for me and I gave him directions to the first store. I wanted to blurt out questions, but I didn't want to seem rude, so I bit my lip and enjoyed the ride. Being chauffeured about in both cars was like riding in a dream. Two hours later, we returned to the office with all my bags and packages. He helped me into the office and after we set things down, I gave him a hug and a kiss for a wonderful morning. I told him how delighted I was and he hugged me tightly. He kissed me passionately, and I could feel that he was aroused, his erection bulging against me through our clothes.

While he kissed expertly, I still was a little apprehensive about Elvis. I didn't know how he could afford to drive such wonderful, expensive cars, and my mind was racing with questions as his hands traveled down my spine and hips. I was being lured into his passion, but I wasn't ready to go so far with him that quickly. Something wasn't right and I couldn't quite place it. My Josaphine detector was on full alert.

He released me and started speaking rapidly in French. I couldn't follow his words at all, but his actions were obvious. He unzipped his pants and released his johnson, shocking and taking me completely off guard. That was the oddest johnson I had ever seen. It was flat headed like a snake, and he was flinging it around in a circle like a cobra ready to strike.

He pointed it at me and asked me to hold it for a minute. I stared at him and then his johnson, still in a state of astonishment. It was so big and flat-ish like a mean looking rattlesnake, and I ran around the desk in the other direction. In a New York minute, Elvis had gone from gentleman with outrageously nice cars, to a grotesque figure waving his johnson at me.

I told Elvis I was not ready for this kind of thing, but he just laughed and waggled his johnson some more, saying, "You can't resist making love to this prince." I ran around the desk again, and he followed like we were running a marathon. I stopped suddenly, panting. Okay, this fruitcake is getting too weird for me. The madness has to stop! I yelled for him to put his "prince" back in his pants and leave my office right now. I picked up my stapler, ready to launch it at his prince. He patted his flathead gently, in a lusty caress.

I'm sure he was about to open his mouth to recover his chances with me. Before he spoke, I snapped out of a state of idiot-ness and realized what he had done; how poorly he had behaved. My decision was clear, and I knew this crazy prince was really a freakin' weirdo who drove "sex machines." I wanted no more to do with him. We hardly knew each other! I had to wonder what else he was capable of doing.

My mind made up, I threw the stapler at him and picked up my tape dispenser, raised and ready for round two. "Out! Out, out, out!" As he left, I yelled for him to never call me again and chased him to the door. "The nerve of that man!" I thought. "Calling his member a 'prince' and expecting me to bow or blow on it!"

Lesson learned– Swank cars are absolutely aphrodisiacs! Throw an African prince in the mix and you've got some heavy-duty attractions! But you have to decide to go with the flow or stay out of those snazzy wheels. A too-expensive ride might be a sign of a freaky mind!

30

GEORGE – THE SECOND OLDER MAN

For a while, I had a part time job in the office of an upscale mall. One day as I passed out the monthly calendar of events to each store, I passed an attractive older gentleman sitting outside of Brooks Brothers. When I came out of the store, he was watching me, so I smiled and said hello.

He asked me if I was new to the mall, and I said I was. He introduced himself as George, the store tailor. He told me he was Jamaican and that he had worked in that store for over twenty years. I hadn't known the mall was that old. He went on to say how lovely I looked, and I thanked him for the compliment and went on about my business.

The next day, George came into the mall office where I worked and asked me to join him for lunch. He was so polite and sweet, I thought there couldn't be any harm and went off to lunch with him. We sat in the mall lobby and watched festive decorations for the holidays going up as we chatted away. After a bit I excused myself, telling him I was going to browse around Filene's, because we were facing the lingerie displays. I saw a silk robe that definitely had my name on it.

He waited and watched as I took the robe off the hanger and felt its creaminess as I held it to my face. It was just gorgeous but, of course, it cost a fortune, way out of my price range. I sadly put it back and tried not to give it another thought. I still hadn't gotten used to being surrounded by a mall full of such lovely things I couldn't afford.

Days and then weeks slipped by with work, and the holidays snuck up on us so quickly, that one day I realized I needed to shop soon or I'd run out of time. I worked through my day looking forward to handling it all in one evening, and as I was about leave the office to get started, I had to stop my plans to handle a delivery. The delivery happened to be for me. My boss was curious, too, that I would be getting mail at our place of business, but I assured her I was just as confused. We agreed it was a bit odd, but I was in a rush and left to get started on my shopping before closing time. I was excited about my mystery package and wanted to open it, and then put it out of my mind. I ran to my car and sat in the driver's seat to tear it open like it was Christmas morning. After taking out loads of tissue paper, my hand brushed against something smooth and creamy. I was simply bewildered! It was the silk robe from the display in Filene's with a card that read, "No need to just look at beautiful things. You should be wearing them. George."

I locked the car and ran back to his store. He was busy taking measurements and doing alterations, so he jotted down his address and asked me to stop by after work. I agreed, with no thought of hanky-panky or romance. It seemed natural because we lived in the same part of town, and he'd been extremely nice to buy something so pretty for me.

I skipped dinner and shopped with a purpose, managing to get a lot done. I couldn't find anything to give George in return. Too soon it was getting late, so I headed for his apartment. The building was a ritzy looking high-rise, and I thought, this older man has some class!

I had the robe with me and started thanking him the moment he opened his door. He smiled and asked if I'd tried it on. On the spur of the moment, I said I wanted him to be the first to see me in it. He laughed heartily and said, "Please show me! I'm honored!"

Josaphine's Lessons

His happiness was infectious, and I found myself sinking fast to his kindness and admiration. I modeled the robe for him, twirling this way and that and doing my best to compete with other models. He gave me a sweet kiss and an appreciative smile, and asked if I was hungry. I said, "Always! And something smells divine." He had fixed island food: curried goat, rice, field peas and corn. He set the table and we sat down to feast. The food was delicious and a real treat for me, since I'd missed eating earlier. As we munched away, he told me that he enjoyed cooking all the time and he promised to make my favorite, which was ox tails with field peas and rice. I told him I couldn't wait.

During the week George sought me out at the mall. We ate lunch together in the lobby as a regular thing and quickly became fast friends. Along the way, I finally found out he was sixty-three. I was less than half his age, but he was so sweet that I found myself attracted to him. I was still taking my time thinking how to proceed with him, when the night for my favorite meal arrived.

I met George at his apartment, and he served me a glass of wine while he set the table. As we were waiting for dinner to finish, we talked and I gave him a present I found to match his generosity. It was a nice pocket watch with a gold chain that linked to his belt. I thought of it as a timeless piece of class, just like George. He seemed very excited and kissed me.

Somehow, the food and wine were forgotten and we started kissing like crazy. He kissed me senseless! His age was a complete non-issue, as I sank into his embrace and enjoyed making out. We made our way to the bedroom where George undressed me and then himself. He looked like he was in good shape. I was warmed up to boiling hot, ready to make George even happier! He placed me on the bed and knelt before me, wanting oral sex. I gladly opened my thighs as he put my legs on his shoulders and began feasting on my nectar. God, that man was talented! I had at least three thrashing, intense orgasms before I realized I had his face in a death grip. My thighs were smothering him! I relaxed, and as he let me go, I felt something foreign come away from his face. I looked up to see one of the strangest things in my life as he recovered his teeth from between my legs! I had squeezed his dentures right out his mouth! As he went to the bathroom to fix his teeth, I came back to my senses about what had just happened. Well, I have to admit that the passion of the moment was lost. I soberly got up and dressed to go home, shaking my head all the while thinking, "Why me, lord?"

George came back to the bedroom and apologized very sweetly, and I assured him it could happen to anybody. Sadly, he and I were over as any kind of romantic "item." I was resolved that that would be the first and last time I let denture cream be mixed with my nectar!

Lesson learned– Think of all the things an older man has to deal with before you engage in sex. The attention, gifts and food might be wonderful, but the age difference might really matter when it comes down to dentures and oral sex!

31

SAMUEL – THE THIRD OLDER MAN

Every morning, whether I was riding the train or driving to work, I stopped at a little café across the street from my job for a coke and a breakfast sandwich. The owners had me pegged as a regular and had my morning package prepared. I saw several people in the café regularly, and one man in particular always smiled at me and said for me to have a great day. I thought little of it, other than as a kind gesture. After seeing him there regularly for a long time, I started looking forward to seeing him, and began thinking of him no longer as a stranger.

One day, I broke the morning-only mold and went in for lunch. Surprisingly, my "have a great day" fellow was there, too, at a table with some other men. Alone, I sat at the counter and wondered if my happy friend was an all-day fixture in the place.

I smiled at the owner and said, "I heard you make a mean Reuben sandwich." He proudly stuck his chest out and told me it was fit for a queen. I ordered one and got comfortable. Looking around, I spotted the men at the table looking me over. It was nice to have the attention, and as I smiled at them, the older gentleman that wished me good morning came over.

"I see you here in the mornings for breakfast," he said in a friendly way. "You work around here?"

"Sure. I work right across the street. I normally don't do lunch," I said, "but today I'm taking care of myself. I'll be working late tonight."

"My name is Samuel."

I was flattered to meet him and told him my name. He took my hand, brought it to his lips and placed a tender kiss on the inside of my wrist. I blushed from his out-of-place, gentlemanly manners! He smiled and told me a lady such as myself was worthy of the highest form of greeting. I thought how sweet he was and what a good looking older man he was, too! I could definitely smell a little something sexy, which made for a heady encounter, but it was briefly over.

The owner came over with my sandwich as Samuel left and added, "You be careful of old Samuel. He's been around this block for years and never misses an opportunity to give, if you get my drift." Chuckling, I thought how perceptive the owner was.

The next morning I was running extremely late and was quite agitated; my day was already in a shambles. I'd spent what had seemed endless, late night hours on a project, only to see it thrown out by the committee. I wasn't a happy camper as I came into the café. Samuel saw me and smiled brightly, and I felt a little tension slip away at the sight of a friendly face.

He came over to me and said, "You look like you had a rough night!" I managed a smile and said, "It's that obvious, is it? You have no idea!" He suggested he might see me for a lunch date at the café and that he looked forward to seeing me feeling better, too, but I couldn't oblige. I asked for a rain check and blew out the door with my morning breakfast, thinking miserably that my food was probably going to be cold by the time I got to eat it.

A week went by in a blur with our office constantly under the gun, and we started having coffee and breakfast from the café delivered to the office. Our projects were all piled up under tight deadlines, keeping us on edge and at each other's throats. By week's end, we'd weathered the storm victoriously, and I felt like I needed some dinnertime R&R.

Josaphine's Lessons

As I left the office and passed by the café, I saw Samuel sitting near the window in his usual seat. He smiled and waved at me to join him, and I went in and sat down. He asked if things were still crazy, and I said I'd gotten past the craziness. Now I needed a relaxing meal and a nice, huge drink. He didn't waste any time with that opening and said, "If things are so much better, you just might be fit company. Let me join you!" He saw that I was a little hesitant and said, "C'mon now—my treat."

I was flattered and *sooo* ready to kick back and be pampered, so we left the café and at his suggestion, headed to an Indian restaurant close by. I had never eaten Indian food, and it was an adventure to experience such tasty and interesting food. I also found it "different" and a little challenging to sit on cushions, cross-legged at a low table.

This was new for me but not for Samuel, and to my delight, he knew just what to order. We had a great meal with several courses, very spicy and topped off with lots and lots of wine. The stress of the week gradually caught up, and tiredness overtook me by the last course. I apologized and told Samuel it was time to go home, even though it was a Friday night, with the weekend off. Samuel took me to my car, opened the passenger side door and told me he was driving me home. He didn't mind catching a cab back. I was a little on the tipsy side and feeling it more, because I was so very tired. I needed to slump into the passenger seat and let him drive me home.

When we arrived at the apartment, I still felt tired, but I wasn't completely ready to hit the sack for the night either. I felt comfortable with Sam and safe enough that I invited him in to continue talking. We were having a good time, and I wanted to get to know him some more. I discovered all my roommates out for the evening, which made me a little anxious, but I decided it was safe enough. In my current state of body and mind, maybe he was the one who should be leery of me!

I had him sit in the den and turned on some music, asking him to wait for me as I took a minute to freshen up. I brushed my teeth, washed my face and changed into a comfortable lounge outfit. I offered him something to drink, but he passed and asked me to sit down next to him. Desire was written across his face, and I knew he wanted to make out. Sam took both my hands in his and came right to the point, saying he wanted to make love to me right now. So much for working into it. "I've ached for you since I laid eyes on you!" This didn't sound corny at all coming from his lips, and I thought, "This man is suh-mooooth!" He grabbed me, held my face, and kissed me like there was never to be another chance. Such amorous kissing melted any reservations. I was truly a goner, intoxicated not just from the wine, but from the heady mix of his aroma, his insistent desire, and his expert and devoted kisses.

When Sam finally let up for a pause, I felt as though I might dissolve in a puddle at his feet. What a kisser! In those few moments, he had taken command of me using only his lips. I was enamored of his whole being, and took that moment to drink in everything about him. I took him to my bedroom, closed the door and sat on the bed. He eyed me with an intensity that relayed his intentions as clearly as a flashing neon sign in the night. Even fully dressed I felt naked. I remember feeling like we were already having sex, even though we'd hardly begun. He bent down to kiss me again. I felt certain I wouldn't be able to take any more kissing at such a superhuman intensity. I felt ready to explode at his next touch anywhere on my body.

He knew what he was doing, and he told me in no uncertain terms that he was going to make me scream with ecstasy all night. For the first time in my life, I was apprehensive by the prospect of having sex with someone who radiated such amazing, sexual intensity! He pulled me closer and whispered soothing words of encouragement. Nothing nasty or dirty, just comforting words to set me at ease, and to increase my wants of something wonderful to come.

As he spoke, he undressed me and gently laid me down. His every move was masterful, like an artist designing a masterpiece. The process was familiar territory for him. He never lost eye contact with me as he took each piece of his clothes off. He was fully erect as he put a condom in my hand and asked me to place it on him. He stated in the sexiest way that we would always practice safe sex. I was impressed that he'd come to the party fully prepared. Not many men I knew were so thoughtful.

Perhaps I should have considered what the chef at the café said, but the thought came and went like a quick breeze. Samuel lay next to me and gave me simple directions, where to place my hands and what he wanted me to do. I followed his directions, wanting to please him as much as he was pleasing me. We caressed, kissed, and joined together with the smoothest entry I have ever felt. He kept the motion slow and the temperature hot. I swayed with him in the slowest dance I could remember. Every inch of movement was ecstasy, and time seemed to slow even more as he asked me to come for him, and do it with lingering release. No rushing it, but just let it flow from me onto him.

He seemed to know exactly what to do moment by moment, how to maximize the feeling of every nerve ending, like some kind of sex guru! My body obeyed him, maximizing the energy being released, and I came in gentle waves. Immediately, he made me release again, this time with him. Our climax mellowed, and I thought I wanted it to never stop, to never come down. Samuel held me tightly while we regained composure to part. We rested for a short while before he took his leave. He'd said "all night long" earlier, and I was so relaxed, sleepy and satisfied that it felt like we made love all night.

Lesson learned– When someone is paying close attention to you, you can believe they are mentally calculating the best way to satisfy you. Sex gurus have it mastered and will impart their knowledge to willing participants. Make sure you are fully energized to endure the encounter for all night. Samuel had a PhD in it!

32

NAMELESS – THE POOL GUY

To work the kinks out of stressful days, I often swam laps in a friend's apartment pool. They had a large, heated, year-round, indoor pool that was perfect for those days when things got out of sorts. I felt the need one day, and squeezed into my spandex swimsuit and headed over to their pool. When I got there, I went in without looking to see if anyone was watching. I took off my robe, put my sandals near a lounge chair and dove in.

The place was often deserted, and I thought I was alone as I started swimming laps. I swam hard, giving my muscles a good workout, and kept going until I was well winded. I turned on my back to breathe and recover in the gentle sway of the water. I opened my eyes to see a man staring at me.

Lost in my laps, I had no idea how long he'd been there. He was obviously the pool guy from the gear in his hands, but he looked at me like I wasn't supposed to be able to swim like a professional. I stopped swimming and asked if I had to get out. He asked me if I'd seen the pool closed sign, which made his odd looks more reasonable. I apologized at once, swearing I didn't notice it. He said he would give me a few more minutes, but that he had to get started soon.

Thanking him, I promised not to take long and lazily started doing some cool-down laps. "Nice looking," I thought to myself, wondering if he was thinking the same thing about me. I knew my full figure was enticing in this $80.00 swimsuit, but as I swam, he had to love the view: nice full body, plus tight black spandex, equals staring in anybody's book! When I got back to the shallow end and stood up, he was there watching and smiling, as though getting a good look was an everyday perk of his job. I was nicely relaxed and didn't care as I rested against the end of the pool to stretch. He came over and made conversation, complimenting my swimming and asking how I learned to swim. I told him about some childhood fun with my brothers and how they taught me. "In a house full of siblings, you learn to swim, or you get pushed under and teased!" I told him.

He admitted he didn't know how to swim and wanted to learn. I was willing to play that little game and smiled, betting myself I could catch him lying about it. What pool guy do you know can't swim? I'm sure he wanted to get close to me and maybe today, I didn't care...!

I responded, "Oh, it's easy. I can have you swimming in no time. Jump in if you want a lesson!" Sometimes, I am not sure about what comes out of my mouth so quickly, especially around men. This time, I was ready to take whatever came and waited to see what he would do. I shouldn't have worried about whether or not he would play! He took off his work clothes slowly, with bumps and grinds, as he got in the pool next to me. I had already developed a different kind of sweat!

But, I simply asked if he could float. "It's the very first thing you have to do." He said he couldn't even do that, and said it with a pretty genuine expression, innocent and blank-faced. I started wondering if he really was unable to swim, and how did he get a job cleaning pools?

Of course, teaching someone how to float requires touching. It's unavoidable. Playing the competent teacher, I told him what I wanted him to do and promised I wouldn't let him sink. When he arched back along the surface into position, I placed my hands under his back and gasped a little at the scorching heat radiating from his well-developed muscles. Good looking and actually hot to the touch, I bit my lip to keep from just massaging him. I forced myself to take a step back and let him go.

Josaphine's Lessons

We tried the float technique for a few minutes, but he said he was impatient to do the next step. I was becoming very excitable by touching him so much. I took him along the edge of the pool until our feet didn't touch the bottom anymore, and demonstrated treading water. He was so calm about it all. I was thinking that either this guy really can't swim, or he is really talented in the acting department, because in my state of mind, I couldn't tell the difference! I wanted him to stay close to the edge of the pool so he could grab it if he started to sink, but he pushed off. He tried, but quickly floundered and reached for me to come help him. All those tight muscles were probably too heavy to float.

He really could need help, I thought, suddenly believing he was clueless in the water and went to help him. I pulled him to the side of the pool, where he suddenly became quite competent and pressed his body full length to mine, kissing me on the lips.

Well, that question is resolved, I thought. What a player! But I played along and innocently asked, "What was that for?" He kept his arm around my waist and said, "For taking the time to show me how to float and tread water, of course." His eyes were mere inches from mine, and they were boring right into me. "Well, that's not the proper way to say, 'thank you,' you know," I said with a hungry appetite.

He smiled and said, "You're the teacher. Why don't you show me?" I took him back to the shallow end where we could stand, but we were still in waist deep water. Teaching time was over for me as he pushed me against the edge of the pool. He kissed me while his hands slid under my suit. I sighed into his mouth and kept kissing as his fingers found the entrance to my womanhood. Finding me ready inside, he swore and crashed into me.

He squirmed out of his swim trunks, eased up between my legs and thrust inside me, holding my swimsuit to the side. I felt a little tear of the material and thought, "Strong! And, oh, so very hard! Hmmm... all that in me!" He pumped and pumped, and I moaned and moaned. He remained in control enough to hold my mouth shut, to cover the scream that welled up from the tips of my toes to the top of my head.

I was ablaze as we found release together. The bubbling energy that started all over my body encased us both, until we slumped down into the water, satiated...we never stopped to consider that someone could walk in on us at any moment.

I dragged my limp body to the edge of the pool and climbed out. Gathering up my things, I left on unsteady legs. I looked back from the door and saw him still watching me. I was sure he wanted to say something, but we were speechless. We took only a moment to look and then waved goodbye. I never even asked the pool guy his name.

Lesson learned– Teaching hard-bodied pool guys to swim is a sinful enough game. If you're invited to give the pool man "lessons," be assured you won't be teaching him anything about how to swim! Just remember to ask his name and remind him how to properly say "thank you!"

33

ROBERT – NOT SATISFIED

The car windows were fogged up, and I was nearly breathless as I tried to get Robert deeper and deeper into me. We were cramped and having a tough time making out in the front seat of my little Honda Accord. I was squirming around on top of him in the passenger seat, when my foot bumped the stick shift out of gear, and the car started to roll forward. Robert grabbed the brake and we pulled apart, which broke the moment. I wanted more of him and he was, of course, not satisfied.

Our next try was on the floor of his new apartment. He hadn't gotten a bed yet, so we stretched out on some pillows and a blanket pallet thrown on the floor. The very unforgiving and uncarpeted floor. I knew I was going to provide the cushioning, so I asked if we could drive across town to my place, but he asked, "What's the matter with the floor?"

My appetite matched his impatience, so I figured we'd make the best of it. The car had been cramped and maybe not so safe. This has to be a big improvement anyway, I thought. Robert lay next to me and began rubbing all over. He was rubbing my stomach when he suddenly stopped and looked straight in my face and asked, "When do you think you can lose some of this?"

I was shocked speechless! What a thing to say and what a horrible time to say it! "What the hell?" was the best I could come up with, and I started pushing away. But, he was quickly on top of me and started kissing me so passionately, that I somehow pushed it out of my head. I was lost in his urgency for the moment, and decided I could think about what to say later.

When the sex was over, it seemed pretty clear that we didn't make anything satisfying happen for either of us. I wasn't very happy feeling like a "wham bam, thank you ma'am," but I sensed he was disappointed in me also. Too tired to argue, I let it go and fell asleep, thinking I'd have some bruises in the morning. During the restless sleep, I got up and went home.

Waiting for Robert to come to my house a few days later, I reflected on our relationship, short as it had been to that point. His comment about my stomach came back to mind, putting me in less than a romantic mood. I hadn't known Robert for long, but already the sex had not been great any of the times we attempted it. Looking back, I realized that we only had, or tried to have, sex in the most unusual places: The car, the floor, and once in what has to have been the smallest shower ever built. My hips hurt just thinking about that tile.

He already told me of his plan to do it on top of my backyard dog house, but I was going to have to draw the line, "adventure" or not. I would be the one with splinters in my butt! All this stuff sounded freaky and kinky coming out of his mouth, right up until the logistics came into play. Somehow, it seemed that "logistics" at best meant someplace uncomfortable, or more likely, me ending up bruised, scratched or smashed. I determined that this unfortunate trend was going to have to end tonight.

Robert was on his way, and I would attempt to get him to have sex in a proper bed. I would have to plan a strategy for every oddball idea he was likely to come up with. My living room was small, nicely done, and quite cozy. But I had an uncomfortable sectional couch, which was not going to be on my "acceptable" list. No way was he getting on top of me in my miniature galley of a kitchen! At least I didn't have a shower, so I thought I could talk him out of doing it in my tub, where there was nothing but a hard, porcelain surface.

Robert showed up with a barbequed chicken pizza and wings for dinner. "Damn!" I thought, "Greasy food again. Maybe he's trying to give me gas! Wouldn't that be stinky?" We ate in the living room while we watched TV. The pizza was surprisingly good but the wings were too hot for my taste. I told him that anything called THREE MILE ISLAND SAUCE was not supposed to be consumed!

After watching a few shows and before my digestion could play any tricks, it was time to put my plan into action. I asked if he wanted to come to bed and started to get up.

"In your bed?"

"Well, yes..."

His "NO!" was emphatic.

"What could possibly be the matter with the bed? We've tried the car, a mini-shower and the floor. Maybe you aren't happy screwing anywhere normal?" I sneered.

He grabbed my hands and pulled me to him, laughing. He kissed my anger away and, in a move I had not foreseen, led me into the sun room, where I had a daybed and some outside chairs. He led me over to the daybed and pushed me down on it, still smiling.

We couldn't fit on the daybed side by side. He had to crouch on top of me to get back to kissing. Within moments I could feel the heat rising between us, and our kisses grew more urgent. He groaned and started moving side to side, stretched out fully on top of me. I felt his erection pressing hard into my stomach through our clothes, and he began to press me harder into the day bed. Our kissing was hot and heavy, but I couldn't move much as I lay pinned beneath him. He fumbled between us and got his erection out through his zipper, and continued to grind and press it against me, his breathing coming harder and harder. I arched up to meet his thrusting motions as much as I could as his passion mounted, and he held me tighter and tighter.

Suddenly, he called my name as he gave one last thrust and released all over my clothes.

There I was, pumped and warmed to fever pitch, left unfulfilled in what I realized was once more an oddball place and release. As he stood up, he told me that was some of the best sex he'd ever had, but that he wasn't really satisfied, and went to the bathroom to clean himself up, leaving me there with a sticky mess. I was totally flabbergasted and outdone! How did my plans get thrown to the wind? This was it for his narrow ass!

No longer stunned, I lay there contemplating ways to disfigure the man. I realized that perhaps, I had been seriously slow to pick up on the signals of this impending failure. I could only conclude that the evening's selfish episode had been the final nail in the coffin for Robert, and his strange ideas of never being satisfied. In no small terms or words, I went to the bathroom and let him know he wasn't the only one unsatisfied in this relationship. I told his narrow ass behind to get to steppin'. We were no longer going to see how unsatisfied we could make each other.

Lesson learned– There is just no excuse for bad sex. If everything you do sexually feels "out of character," and you get no satisfaction the first time, the second time or the third time, it's time to "get a clue." Kinky and freaky might be interesting for some, but in the end honey, you deserve to get some satisfaction, too! AMEN.

34

LEROY – THE STOP-OVER MAN

Living in the South takes some getting used to, and having friendly folks "stop over" unannounced is an example. Living in the North, I was used to people calling before they came over. Leroy was one hundred percent southern in that respect, liable to stop by anytime without warning.

Much to my delight, he was also sensual, sex-craved, and delicious; my "Stop-Over Man!"

On a pretty day not long after moving south, I was resting at a picnic table between classes at the school where I was substituting, debating with myself whether to have lunch outside. My mind was made up for me when a man in a school maintenance shirt came out into the courtyard, looked at me and smiled. He was carrying a sheet of glass, and I glanced behind him to notice some nearby broken windows. He put the glass down and measured the window, reaching up, down and across, stretching himself out. The view outside is nicer, I thought, with my mind made up about where to sit for lunch. I put my drink down and did some of my own measurements, scoping out the length of his legs, and the shape of his butt, which was nicely outlined in his work pants.

He turned and caught me looking and laughed. He stopped working and walked over, asking if I was new. I told him that I was new to both the area and the school. He introduced himself as Leroy, and I laughed before I could catch myself. I quickly apologized and said I'd never met anyone whose was actually named Leroy. "How could that be? There's Leroy's everywhere!" he said. "Well, it isn't a common name where I'm from up North," I explained. "And my name's Josaphine." He gave my laugh right back to me, and said my name wasn't so common for a black lady in the South, either. Touché!

He asked what part of town I was living in. I told him where I was staying and he said he knew that area well, and asked if he could stop by if he was ever in that part of town. I was a little surprised that he might think to stop over unannounced any old time, but I chalked it up to meaningless chit chat. I didn't think much of it and didn't give him my number, but I wondered to myself if Southern folks "just dropped by" all the time.

After meeting Leroy, I didn't work for a few days while school was out, and enjoyed sleeping in and lounging around my little house. I was watching movies one afternoon when Ralph, my big, ugly-headed, dog-slash-automatic-doorbell jumped up and started barking. I peeked out the peep hole and recognized none other than Leroy. He'd really meant it!

I opened the door, and he smiled and asked if I had any coffee. "Well, that's interesting, Leroy, because it's the middle of a hot afternoon, and I don't drink coffee," I said. Didn't faze him at all. He stared at my crazy, mismatched, but somewhat sexy outfit and asked if I was going to let him in.

"I don't think so, Mr. Leroy!" I said, "I wasn't expecting company and the house is a mess."

He laughed and said to pay it no mind because he wouldn't look at anything but me.

"Flattery will get you everywhere," I said, letting Ralph out and Leroy in. As he stepped into my small living room, I swear there was a familiar coziness, like he was right at home. He sat down like he'd been coming over for years. I sat down on the couch next to him and restarted the movie.

Josaphine's Lessons

Of course, a love scene was just getting under way. "Great timing, movie!" I muttered under my breath and laughed a little. It must have been the cue he needed. He asked what I thought was so funny while he slid closer to me and danced his fingers along the back of my shoulders.

Like a synchronized watch, my body started signaling green lights, and I let out a little happy moan. He saw the invitation and followed up his first exploration with a full blown journey, further down my back and around to my hips. Meeting no resistance, he began roaming all over my body, shamelessly mirroring the hot action in the movie. I couldn't help thinking what perfect timing my movie had been for his visit. Yes, yes, me too on the synchronized timing. So perfect, I wanted to scream because it felt so good! I was quivering with delight and we hadn't even kissed! I wasn't dressed for entertaining, much less enticing sex. My place was a wreck. I hardly knew him. He didn't care and very quickly I didn't either. The moment he kissed me, any thought of slowing down was gone. He suppressed my moans with his kisses and laid me back on the couch.

His hands were everywhere, massaging my boobs and rubbing my thighs through my clothes. I was rapidly getting "hotter than a burning bush" and wanted my t-shirt and pajama bottoms off. He sensed my desire and took my shirt off and then my pants. He feasted his eyes on me and, oddly I thought, how glad I was that I'd brushed my teeth. Thank God we can't read each other's minds. Of all the things I could think about, weird stuff sometimes goes through my head in the heat of the moment.

My next thought was spent wishing he was just as naked. I said it with my eyes, I guess, as he stood upright on cue, took off his shirt and tossed it aside. He then lustfully thrust his hips toward me, took my hand and placed it on the front of his bulging pants. I caressed his hardness and cupped my hand around him, and there was so much heat, I jerked back amazed. He put his hand on top of mine and caressed my hand over his delight, over and over again to the sway of his hips. I quickly got more and more excited from his erotic dance, until I could feel myself getting wet in the necessary area. Unable to resist any more, I opened his pants and released his dancing member, dropping his pants to the floor. He stepped out of them, and we came together flesh to flesh, dancing in a slow circle around the small living room.

The bedroom loomed closer, and he danced me through the door to my rumpled bed where we tumbled together, embracing. Our "dance" shifted to a different step, as he turned me over and spooned me against his body. He started humming in a way that was close to a moan but interestingly different. His moaning turned to words, a stream of nasty hot words, spilling in my ear. I was entranced, and pushed my bottom back arching toward him. His fingers found the entrance to my delight and made their own wild rhythm. I closed my eyes and swayed to their beat. I moaned as he said more and more nasty things about what he wanted to do, until I lost all common sense. I agreed to his spoken words and his rhythm, pushing my reply against him. He slipped inside me from behind and pinned me tighter to him. We began a tempo dictated by nature, with my face buried in the bed and my hands grabbing the sheets. He was so filling, so demanding, that my passion and urgency escalated to match his. My breathing and movement, the scandalous feeling of him inside me, filled my brain to overflowing. We danced that cadence steadily for a few ecstatic minutes, and then began to build up and up and up until we ended in a shattering lightening. Panting and recovering, I turned around, and we lay side by side looking at each other. He smiled and caressed me, saying he was glad he stopped by today.

"You never know, I just might be in this area again sometime. Would it be all right if I stop over again soon?"

I simply said with a lusty smile, "Anytime!"

Lesson learned– The stop-over man is a good incentive to keep yourself and your house in "anytime" order. You might not need to make the bed, though, because it's going to get messy!

35

JAMES – THE TIRE MAN

One day my car had a flat tire on a side of town I wasn't familiar with, and I called for assistance. The mechanic who showed up was grimy from working the tow truck, I supposed, but very dark and handsome. It was easy to see how sexy he was, and his hard work only made him more attractive. I enjoyed watching him fix my tire and that would have been that, but he inspected the others and showed me how bare the treads were. He offered to tow the car back to his shop and fix me up for a really good price. I was naturally frustrated to spend the money, but of course, needed the car for work, so on to the tire shop we went.

When we reached the shop, James assisted me down from the truck. His truck had been a gross and smelly experience, and I was happy to be done with the discomfort. Otherwise, the ride and conversation had been pleasant. James and I had talked and laughed the entire way. He could tell I wasn't from around these parts. My New England accent had been a dead giveaway and I wasn't in any mood to hide it, frustrated about my car and talking faster than the speed of light. We chatted about getting to know a new place; finding your way around, making do when trouble comes around and so forth, and I found him surprisingly well-spoken.

He showed me to a not-so-very-clean waiting area, while he found the tires I needed and got to work. He was in the process of changing a tire, when I looked out and spied him squatting down by the front tires. He had a strong back and very strong looking legs. He was a gorgeous hunk of man, but covered in grease and sweat from head to toe. I had to use my imagination. As I continued to enjoy the view, my mind skipped past his grime and was lost in fantasy. I was doing all kinds of imaginary things with his muscular body, when he looked towards me and winked. Well, you would think I felt embarrassed, but I just winked back and saluted him.

What was I thinking? He was a muscular grease spot, and I had to admit that I couldn't stop thinking about how magnificent he'd be all cleaned up. James finished up and after I paid, he smiled broadly and said I should call him some time. I didn't give it any serious thought, but while driving home, I found myself still trying to get my fantasy-fixated mind off his rippling muscles. I was chatting to myself, when I suddenly found out that I would be calling him sooner than even my sex-crazed imagination could have foreseen. The original flat tire had gone flat again. "DAMMIT," I shouted, as I pulled carefully into my driveway.

I immediately called James at the shop, but he didn't answer. That figures! I thought, feeling a little like I'd been set up for a rotten afternoon. By late evening, I still hadn't been able to reach the shop and was getting worried. Without my car, I would have a real problem in the morning getting to work, and I simply had to get it fixed. I called again, praying for James to pick up, but the answering machine came on with a message saying the shop was closed. I was so angry; I started to leave a very unladylike message, when James picked up. I was caught off guard when he was so nice that I apologized quickly, changing my tone to become the desperate lady in distress. He calmed me down by saying he'd come over as soon as he could, so I gave him my address and returned to my cooking, thankful that a solution was in the works.

Josaphine's Lessons

By the time he arrived it was well into the evening, but the problem proved stress free as he fixed the tire easily. When James came to the kitchen to let me know he was done, we chatted a bit. At one point he asked if I lived alone, and I nonchalantly said, "No, I live with Ralph," and watched his eyes to see what I'd get for a reaction. I got a smile out of it as my big-headed, lab mix, Ralph, heard his name and joined us in the kitchen, barking and wagging his tail for some attention. James laughed and took to Ralph, too, saying his name and petting him. Ralph happily flopped onto the floor for a belly rub, and James complied, rubbing his stomach and saying, "I bet that feels good!" Ralph happily responded by shaking his leg in tune to the rubbing. James stood and paused, smiling, and told me the smell of my cooking was driving him crazy. I took the not-so-subtle hint and asked if he could stay for dinner, saying there was going to be plenty. I invited him to clean himself up before we sat down, so he went to his car for a change of clothes and showered. "Always prepared for the damsel in distress," I thought. "How convenient!"

When I put a plate of lamb and red beans with rice in front of him, James declared he was in heaven. Ralph joined us, demanding some as well, so I put some bones in Ralph's plate and joined James at the table. Considering our earlier chat, I wasn't surprised when we had a delightful evening and got along really well, joking and teasing through dinner. This has some potential, inviting him to stay and relax for a while. We retired to the living room, and just as we got comfortable and turned on the TV, there was a knock on the door. Leroy, my Stop-Over Man, had stopped by in time to squelch my prospects with James. He must have intruding-on-my-space radar.

Oh, shit! What the hell do I do now? Thankfully, Leroy was civilized when he saw James on the couch, and they shook hands as he sat down. I explained James' visit for the car, and as I sat between them, my body made up my mind for me. Leroy had my body humming from the moment I opened the door, and he made my body sing, tremble, and pulsate; so, I knew the unknown James would have to remain a grease spot for a while. James adjusted easily to the situation and simply enjoyed relaxing through the rest of the TV show. When the show went off, I walked James to the door and thanked him, and he promised to check on my tires and me the next day. I could tell James wanted to have his chances too, which was fine with me. I didn't say anything to lead him on, but I wasn't an exclusive with Leroy and left things open with James.

When I returned, Leroy was off the couch and heading to the bedroom with a bit of heat in his step. Wondering how he was, I went in to find him almost undressed and moving fast. He tossed his pants aside and grabbed me for a forceful kiss. "This might not be half bad," I thought! He stopped the kiss abruptly to tear my clothes off and threw me on the bed. He finished undressing and came close, strutting and reaching for me to come to him. Leroy was hotter and harder than I could remember, and I was vibrating like a tuning fork and seeing double. Observing the result of apparent competition, I decided that the competitive, beastly approach had its worth!

I thought he would start talking nasty to heat me up, but all he said was, "You're mine, you're mine." I could hardly breathe as he pulled me into a vise grip, sucking on my boobs and fingering me expertly to an orgasm in record time. Giving me no time to recover, he shoved me against the headboard, lifted my legs up over his shoulders and shoved into me in one long stroke. He pounded into me like nothing else mattered, bouncing me against the headboard like a basketball. All I could do was take it, thinking I was going to have bruises everywhere, and my neck was going to be sore from whiplash. He was a man with a purpose, as he took me from pain to pleasure, pain to pleasure—and finally, to a pinnacle of roaring, explosive pleasure. I thought one of us just might bust a blood vessel.

After we climaxed, he was sweating and breathing heavily, and I felt like I'd hit a brick wall after running a marathon. Both of us were completely spent. We looked at each other and he mumbled, "Mine!" I nodded and whispered, "Yours." We fell onto the bed looking for sleep like limp rags, absolutely done. The "Stop-Over Man" was no more as Leroy was promoted, on the spot, to "Constant Companion." James would service my tires and Leroy would service me.

Lesson learned– The possibility of sexual prowess in the men you meet is nice, but if you have a lion by the tail already, keep pace with him and let the other studs you see walk on bye. But, dangling the prospect of competition in front of your lion, might get you to be the queen of the pride.

36

MARK – SPECIAL LITTLE FRIEND

After years of experience, I felt sure very few men could surprise or overwhelm me; but, Mark proved to be a special case.

I met Mark through a network of party going friends, when he started getting to know some folks in the group. As the only single woman in the group, I was always being set up with single men, and when someone introduced him to me, I wasn't surprised. At first sight, he was so incredibly sexy. I was actually suspicious of going out with him. I knew going out with someone who looked better than you could prove very dangerous. I was deliberately slow in getting to know him. He practically oozed sexiness and was built like a romance novel cover stud. His presence was practically overwhelming, and I probably would have just run away, except that I found him unexpectedly easy going and easy to talk to; and I liked challenges...

Everyone in the group liked him as well, so I decided to get to know him better. We chatted at gatherings for a while here and there and we, over time, became friends. He wasn't conceited or pushy and was really down to earth and honest. I found out that he was unattached and fairly new to town, trying to find his way. We exchanged numbers without any commitment, other than to talk more over the next few weeks. We conversed between social gatherings until we finally set up a date for the coming weekend.

Early Saturday morning before our date, I got a frantic call from him. He said he was sorry to impose, but he was feeling really sick and needed somebody to help him. I offered to come to his place, but he said he was already out at breakfast. He hadn't been able to finish his meal and was feeling too awful to make it through the day alone. Catching a cab, he soon dragged himself into my place. I could tell at a glance that he was sick as a dog, and when I felt his forehead, I was certain he had a fever and maybe the flu. From the way he was talking, he must have been half delirious.

I ran through options: If it's the flu, a doctor is no real help; hospital is the same and costs more; and, home alone would be beyond miserable. I knew he had no one to look after him, so I insisted he wasn't going anywhere. My place was just a one bedroom, but it would have to do. "This is not how I thought I'd get to know Mr. Sexy," I pondered, as I took him straight to my king-size bed.

I fed him some pain reliever with fever reducer and guided him to a shower to cool his skin down. With a little smile, he asked me to join him. I told him he could hardly stand up, and to slow all that masculinity down. He really needed to rest. I wasn't beyond looking at the show as he started unabashedly shedding clothes, but I forced myself to retreat back to the kitchen and make him some chicken broth.

Through the bedroom door, I heard him collapse onto the bed, and when I checked on him, he was stark naked and spread out across it, damn near taking up the whole thing. Lovely sight, indeed, but I bit my lip and quietly murmured, "He's sick, he's sick, he's sick." I could only sigh with regret and focus on making him some soup and a hot toddy. The faster he's better.... This brought a wicked smile to my face, and I got to work immediately.

As I set the tray down, he sat up and wanted me to feed him. If this god-like specimen is so in need of mothering, I thought, that's fine with me! I got him some Nyquil and fed him soup, a spoon at a time. I made a pair of hot toddies and we toasted to good health. In minutes, he was back to fully being horizontal and fast asleep, literally passed out.

Josaphine's Lessons

I left a note for Mark in case he woke and ran some errands, stopping along the way to see the couple who introduced Mark to our group. I joined them in a late brunch and told them what was going on, generating smiles and snickering from them, and blushing from me. Using the "but he's so sick!" defense just earned me some more friendly chuckles with raised eyebrows. They said they knew it was coming to this, and I told them we had planned a date, but I didn't want it to be quite like this!

I returned after brunch to the sound of snoring still coming from the bedroom. I was glad Mark was sleeping so his body could heal, and he slept very soundly for the rest of the day and into the night. I washed his clothes, set them out and settled down to enjoy one of my many romance novels.

When he finally woke up and joined me in the living room, Mark said he felt better and very rested. I told him how long he had been out, and he moaned and held his head in his hands, cursing that he missed going to work. Although it was Saturday and late, he called his job to report in, and they told him to get better, that it wouldn't be a problem. I couldn't resist asking, "Where do you work?" Funny, how in all our conversations, that detail never came up.

He told me he did some part-time work at a nightclub, inviting me to come and see him sometime. Bartender made sense, and I said I would definitely come out to his place. We talked some more, ate sandwiches and soup, with more medicine for his dessert, and then watched a movie. His flu symptoms seemed to be much better, but he was still tired and sniffy. We cuddled our way through a full movie when he started to doze again.

I got him back to the bedroom, helped him undress (my, my, my, what a chore) and put him back to bed. Grabbing some sheets for the couch, I realized this made the second time in one day that I had a man in my bed without jumping in with him. Sigh! Double sigh!!

The next morning I made pancakes and eggs with hot tea and honey, which Mark gobbled enthusiastically. His powers of recovery were amazing. With his symptoms the day before, I bet myself no one else I knew would have been so energetically up and around. But he was feeling much better with no sniffles, refusing pain killers, and asked me to take him to his home and hang out there. He was delighted when I agreed to spend the day with him.

We went to the apartment he rarely shared with two other guys, but no one was around. He showered and changed, coming out in his uniform of a t-shirt and sweat pants. He was looking like a pretty healthy chunk of anatomy from my point of view, something that stepped right out of "GQ." Distracted, I didn't register a thing he talked about. I thought if I watched him walk around in front of me long enough, I probably would just lose it. Give me a few minutes, some one-way glass and a couch, and I could probably reach a climax just looking at all that.

I was getting highly aroused just being near him. Afraid that I'd start acting like a dog drooling over a bone, I tried to get a grip and act like a normal woman in spite of myself. I tried. My brain was at war with itself. "That's not going to happen," the left side of my brain said. "You can't stay in the normal person category with this *super sexy mortal* parading around at arm's length." The right side of my brain volunteered, "Just don't say anything. You can't mess up if you shut up; just put us on hold."

The left side won, hands down. I resolved that the first chance I got, I was going to pounce all over that body—no doubt, no holds barred, and sooner rather than later. The last straw in my internal argument was that he seemed recovered. No hacking, no sniffles; healthy. It's time to turn off momma mode and to begin my personal agenda.

We talked more, and he thanked me again and again for taking care of him. He bent over me and gave me a kiss. Ahh haah! The opening I was looking for. I pulled him down on top of me and he came willingly. We made out on the couch for a long time. He kissed me with the expertise I knew he had, until I was half breathless and on the brink of ripping our clothes off. Coming up for air, he paused and invited me to his room. I would have happily done it on the floor.

Mark's room was definitely male, saturated with matching smells. I was in heaven with the aroma. On autopilot, I took off my clothes and got into bed. Mark was messing with some box under his bed, and asked me to be still for a minute and close my eyes. I followed his direction, anticipating what we would soon be doing to each other, when he quietly said, "I want you to meet my special little friend. Open your eyes."

I laughed because I knew his "little friend" was far from little, and slowly opened my eyes expecting to see his special friend in my face. Instead, I instantly screamed and moved as fast as lightening to the other side of the room. He had the largest snake I'd ever seen wrapped around his neck and some of his body. It was slithering around and he was caressing it. I shouted, "Neeegro! What the hell is that thing? Holy shit, Mark!" and clutched a pillow for cover.

"Relax, woman; she's perfectly safe. I've had her for years. She's part of my act. Sassy hasn't eaten and I've got to feed her." Lord, lord, lord, it was enormous—bigger around than his arm. My pre-determined orgasm was visiting another hemisphere, and if someone had brushed me with a feather, I'd have jumped through the ceiling. My mind was trying to process the rush of information as he put "Sassy" in a big aquarium and went into the kitchen. "Part of his act?" What kind of act was he performing? Was he with a circus? What have I gotten myself into this time, dammit?

I couldn't believe he left me in the room alone with a monster snake, and my eyes stayed glued to it; feet ready to move. It was looking at me like it was calculating how to swallow me whole. She could survive for months on a body as big as mine. My ass alone would feed her for a month, I thought. I became frozen to the wall after I backed away from the glass cage. Mark came back to the room with a white box. It was moving. I watched, transfixed, as he took out two little mice and put them in with the snake. "Watch," he said, and I found that I couldn't tear my eyes away, even though I was repulsed at the same time.

That snake must have been hungry, swallowing those poor little mice in one fast motion each, sucking them down with no noise, no mess. Gone as though they'd never been. They didn't stand a chance. "That's just disgusting!" I picked up my clothes and fled from the room, still naked. Mark followed me out and asked me what was wrong. "It's completely natural...."

"Don't you find it a little strange to have a snake in your bedroom?" I interrupted.

Mark went to touch me and I slapped his hand away. He had snake slime on him or something; I didn't want him to touch me. I wasn't afraid, but as I put my clothes back on, I was definitely getting angry. He asked me to sit down and let him explain. The snake was a part of his act. He was an erotic dancer at the famous Magic City Club downtown. I was shocked, but it all added up. I bet he made a lot of money taking his clothes off. I had to admit, I'd put a few twenties in his G-string any day. But the snake was just over the edge for me; he was way too friendly with it.

He suggested we get dressed and go back to my place and I readily agreed, very ready to be well away from that anaconda. We went for a long ride and talked about it. He apologized for springing Sassy on me that way, and I told him how badly he scared me. It didn't take long before he had me laughing about it. "I'm never going to forget the look on your face. Never!" he swore, laughing. We both had a good laugh when I told him about the not-so-little-friend I was expecting when I'd opened my eyes.

By the time we made it back to my house, I was thoroughly calmed. We were both recovered; him from his flu, and me from my shocking snake discovery. I didn't waste any more time with idle chit chat. As soon as the door locked, I enticed him into a private strip tease as we made our way to my safe, very snake-free bedroom, where I successfully rode his "elongated snake friend" all night long.

Lesson learned– Nurse your man back to health before you ride his *special* friend for the night. Beware of snakes hidden under the bed. Your strip tease man can perform with his different kind of snake that won't scare the hell out of you.

37

LI – THE ASIAN MAN

I now know that arranged marriages still happen in many cultures. I didn't think they existed anymore until I met Li.

I was picking up a call-ahead pizza one evening, when a good looking Asian man came into the store behind me for his own pick up. The second thing I noticed was how tall he was. His shiny black hair was cut fashionably, and he looked as though he had been in the sun all his life. Something about his looks threw me off; I couldn't quite put my finger on it. He spoke with a slight, Asian accent as he checked on his order and sat next to me on a bench while we waited. He exchanged smiles with me pleasantly, but before I could say hello, my name was called to pick up my order. When I opened the box to check my pizza, I immediately said that it wasn't mine. The pizza had anchovies on it, and I ordered a stuffed meat lovers.

The tall, Asian man brushed passed me and said that was probably his. They confirmed it was, so he paid for it and left. In the brief moment we'd been side by side, he smelled delicious. I could remember how he smelled even over the powerful aroma of the pizza. A few minutes later, I finally got my order and left for home.

As I got out of the elevator and juggled around for my keys, the apartment door across from me opened, and Mr. Yang looked out. "Ahhhh," he said, "I thought that was you. You have pizza! Smells good!" I laughed and asked if he wanted some. Mr. Yang was a great neighbor and I liked him a lot. We joked that he was an emergency store for me when I ran out of coffee, sugar, and sometimes food. He often saved me with a smile, and I happily paid him back with thankful appreciation. But tonight, he said no because he was waiting for his son. He held the pizza for me while I opened the door and I said, "I didn't know you had a son." He said he had several children back home in China, but this son was very special. He brought the pizza into the apartment for me and noticed my fish tank was empty.

"What happened to the fish?" he asked. I told him how I had been away on a trip and when I returned, they were dead. He scolded and told me I should have let him help out. I said I was sorry, and sorry for him too, because he was so far from his children, when I heard a knock on my open door.

It was Mr. Yang's son, the tall, Asian man from the pizza parlor, standing with his pizza in one hand and beer in the other. Mr. Yang ran to the door to greet his son. The coincidence was too interesting! Mr. Yang introduced his son as Li, and I invited them to stay. They happily came in and we had a fun dinner together, laughing and talking about everything and nothing. By the time Mr. Yang had gotten to the end of his second beer, I could only understand about a third of what he was speaking, no matter how closely I paid attention. As I struggled to figure out what Mr. Yang was saying, I noticed Li staring at me and smiling in a sexy kind of way. I smiled back at him and searched for something to say. Finally, I asked, "You're so interesting looking! You look Asian, but—not all?"

He laughed and told me he was a little bit of everything, that his mom had been a mallato. After he and his father exchanged a few words in Chinese, Li opened up again and told me more. He spoke of how his dad had been very much in love with her, but they couldn't marry. The sadness in Mr. Yang's face confirmed the story. Li said he was the result of their love, and she died soon after giving birth. So the story began to come together; he had never known his mother and had grown up here in the states, originally cared for by his mother's parents until Mr. Yang found him years later. His half-brother and sisters were still in China with his dad's wife; a whole Chinese family. Li's long delay in being reunited with his father was the result of an arranged marriage that had prevented his parents from marrying, and stopped his father from taking care of him as a young child. I listened, completely entranced by the complexity and tragedy of it. The whole thing was foreign to me in a very sad way.

I told Li I had known his dad for a long time, and asked how come I hadn't met him before. "I did a school internship in Virginia and now that it's done, I have to go with my dad to China for an arranged marriage of my own," he said. I was shocked again, more so this time. This time it wasn't some oddity from decades past. This time it was their lives, their future, here and now.

I couldn't help blurting out, "You? An arranged marriage for you? You weren't born in China! You have to be kidding, right?" Li told me it was true, and Mr. Yang nodded. Li told me that his marriage was a different sort of agreement, something closer to repaying a debt. Mr. Yang tried to explain, too, emphasizing how huge the debt was. I didn't know what to say except for, "When do you have to leave?"

"In a few days. As soon as we can clear up some legal matters, Dad and I will move permanently back to China."

I was still rolling with the shocks, and the story seemed to be getting more bizarre with every new tidbit revealed. This is the 21st century, my mind was saying, when Mr. Yang looked at me with a sad smile and a knowing look as our eyes met for a moment. He stood up to leave but waved his son back, telling Li to stay and enjoy my company. I walked Mr. Yang to the door. He put his arm around me as we went and whispered to me that he wanted his son to laugh and have fun while they were still in America. "China," he said, "will be very, very different. I know what it will be like. Hard. Very hard for Li." He patted me gently, smiled and gave me another of those penetrating looks, then went into his apartment. For a moment I watched the closed door across the hall, trying to take it all in.

Mr. Yang was no longer my next-door food locker. We were connected; and he was now genuinely my friend and neighbor. I still didn't quite understand the whole story, but I knew enough to know it was an inescapable contract, something very serious that touched whole families on the far side of the world. The "debt" that Mr. Yang and Li were paying was incomprehensibly strange, enormous, and very hard to digest.

I pulled Li to the couch and asked if he wanted to watch a movie. He said no, but to put one on if I wanted. I suggested we could just talk for a while and didn't meet any resistance. I put on some low jazz, poured some wine and sat down with him. All the laughter had gone from his intriguing features. I began to realize that by pulling the story out, I had made Li's evening only more morose, and so I resolved to be as comforting as I could.

I was fascinated and couldn't help but look at him. Li really was quite handsome, and his coloring was like mocha chocolate ice cream. I could see how people would perceive him as simply odd looking or weird. He caught me staring and glared back hard to make me aware that I was staring. I simply looked at him like he was a nut and stuck my tongue out at him. We both laughed, breaking the tension.

We drank more wine, and he opened up a bit more. Li told me he didn't want to go to China, much less marry someone he didn't know. His marriage was some kind of hugely serious, decades-old contract between families; a deal that required the illegitimate son to cancel an enormous family debt. He was the final payment. I touched his shoulder and asked him if such things couldn't be dissolved. Only if he fell in love and married in America, Li revealed. If he did that, the debt would be unforgivable, and his family would be destitute for years to come.

He talked about how mistreated he'd been in school for being "different," and how he'd never come close to finding someone he could marry. He said he was petrified to even try, knowing it would cause so much misery. He described how he didn't feel Chinese, and in spite of being raised by his maternal grandparents, he obviously didn't feel American either. I didn't cry, but the violins were playing as Li continued to pour out his heart. My heart had been crushed for him in the short time we were talking, but he had to live with this his whole life!

I asked him if he shared any of these feelings with his dad, and he gave a most emphatic "No." His father had been very good to him, and if this was what was needed, then he would do what was asked of him, no matter the price. Still not really able to wrap my head around the inflexibility of the situation, I said, "Since when does a man loving and taking care of his son come with so high a price?" Li shrugged his shoulders in defeat and put his head in his hands. He looked in total agony. I wasn't repairing anything. I knew I had to find a way to change the direction.

Tonight, Li didn't want to be a student, a son or an outsider. He just wanted to be cared for in his unhappiness. I reached for his hand and rubbed it softly. He leaned back on the couch and asked for more wine. I knew he needed more than a drink, however, and slid closer to him. I didn't think twice about kissing his full lips, and he didn't hesitate long before pulling me closer to him. Our kiss was somewhat slow and urgent all at the same time. He pulled me across his lap, cupped my face with his hands and got more serious about kissing. He was starving for affection, and I could feel him wanting the love that had escaped him for what seemed a lifetime. It wasn't long before I was ready to offer more.

Li and I walked to the bedroom and undressed silently. I was no stranger to sex; this was comfort I could give. We stood naked next to the bed and he looked at me, exploring my full-figured curves. He touched my hair and ran his fingers down my face to my throat. He traced the shape of my breast and then smoothed his hands over my belly and large hips. No words were needed as the air filled with sexual readiness, and Li slid his hand between my thighs to cup my mound. As he massaged me gently, I kept pace and began to moan and grind against his hand. He kissed me again, confirming a natural gift for it, and I found my knees turning to jelly. I grabbed his shoulders, thinking, "How embarrassing it would be if I fell to the floor in a wet puddle?"

He guided me to the bed and we descended together moaning, and kissing, and touching in a frenzied state. When he finally spoke again, his voice was deeper, more urgent, as he told me he wanted, needed to be inside me. He moved above me, placed his aching strength at my entrance, and then cried out as he plunged into me.

He held me tighter and pulled my hips up as he moved into a kneeling position. I woke to my own demands and clutched at him, my legs pulling him as hard as I could into my sweetness, deeper and deeper. He looked at me eye to eye and started moving faster and faster. I stayed locked in his intense eye contact as he drove into me over and over again, pumping in time to his moans of intense and urgent pleasure. I kept time with him, wanting it just as badly, by pulling and squeezing him with everything I had, until he spilled his life source into me with a vigor that resulted in us both shaking and trembling. We collapsed on the bed in a heap of sweat, embracing, holding on as the slow moving air calmed and cooled us. We were quiet again for a long time, smiling and looking at each other eye to eye in the dim light.

It had been enough. No commitments, no bonds, just relaxing in the truth that our sexual encounter had been comforting and satisfying to each other. We pulled the covers up and drifted off to sleep, warm, knowing we would enjoy each other again in the time we had together.

Just a few days later, they were gone. It took a good solid cry for me to start my recovery. Hugging them both goodbye was one of the hardest partings of my life.

Lesson learned– Perhaps there are times when you can make a difference in someone's life without physically doing much. But there may also be times you have to engage all of your mind, soul and body to make the difference in comforting someone. Be assured that when you give yourself completely, you'll be making a memory to last a lifetime.

38

HENRY – THE DETECTIVE

One evening, I came home to chaos, with police cars lighting up the front of my building. The police had a man in the back of a patrol car, and I looked in but didn't recognize him. I found my upstairs neighbor in the lobby with another policeman, and he told me he was pretty sure someone had broken into my apartment. He heard glass shatter in the hall, saw my door open through his peephole and called the police. Luckily, they apprehended the thief in the act.

A policeman confirmed it was my place, and I found out the burglar had been caught loading my new TV and VCR in the back of his car. He had also been caught with several pieces of jewelry. The officer told me my huge dog had been found locked in the office, which made me think it had been an inside job, and that someone had helped him. Ralph wouldn't have gone quietly into the office for a stranger, I was sure.

One of the officers told me to expect a visit from a detective shortly, so I went upstairs to check on things and see if my neighbor was alright. He was fine and thankful that he stayed home from work, completely by chance. He stayed home with a bad headache and had been extra sensitive to noise. The sound of the glass breaking in our shared hallway had immediately gotten his attention. I thanked him profusely; promising him a home cooked meal, and went to take care of my place.

The feeling was awful and only got worse, as I surveyed my violated apartment. Glass was all over the entry, my things gone, ripped from their home. I was shaken, feeling vulnerable and alone, and I knew I had to find a friend. The neighbor who called the police was leaving, and the neighbors living under me weren't home. I cleaned up the remaining glass, fed and cared for my wonderful Ralph, and called everyone I knew who could come and stay with me for a while; but, found no one available.

There was a knock at the door and I about jumped out of my skin. Ralph barked maddeningly, not wanting to share his home with anyone tonight. I grabbed a baseball bat out of complete paranoia and peeked through the broken glass to see two men in suits, one black and one white. Opening the door I asked what they wanted, and they both held up badges for me to inspect. "Detectives Johnson and Murray, Miss. May we come in?"

Relieved, I let them in while holding back Ralph, and we sat in the den. Just back from work, I was still dressed in an outfit that I knew showed off my assets nicely, and I didn't miss Detective Johnson checking me out. Perhaps I should have been a quivering wreck, but I had calmed down a lot and had no problem admiring the gentlemen before me. "How nice of the police department to send me their finest!" I thought. Detective Murray had gorgeous red hair, unfortunately matched by a wedding band. Cute, but married, uninterested and bored; just here to fill out the paperwork. Detective Johnson on the other hand, looked ready to pounce if given the go ahead. Tall, dark and handsome, with a badge to boot. "He can handcuff me any day!" I thought, warming up to him. I didn't have to bat my eyelashes; I could tell he was in the game.

They finished their paperwork, and as I walked them out, Detective Johnson lagged behind. I asked him innocently if there was anything else I could help him with, and he replied, "I get off work in about two hours. I would love to take you for a drink." I had to smile.

This was playing out very nicely indeed! "Why Detective Johnson, I'm sure I don't know you well enough to go out drinking!"

He winked at me and smiled sweetly. "I'm easy to get to know, Josaphine."

"Really; what's your first name, then, Detective? I whispered.

"Henry." He smiled again.

"So Henry, what time will you pick me up?"

"I'll see you at eight, if that's all right."

He had earned a winning smile from me, and whether he knew it or not was already helping me feel like everything would be alright.

"Until then, Henry," I whispered.

As he went downstairs, I saw the victory smile he gave his partner. The situation was so odd, I asked myself out loud, "What the hell am I doing?" I then ran to the bedroom to find something to wear. Ralph was hot on my trail, picking up on my excitement. Getting ready for Henry somehow brought my evening under control, and I made good progress straightening things up. I also got refreshed and ready.

Henry was a pleasant surprise in both character and humor, not at all the starched detective I'd seen "on the job." He was pleasant and entertaining, and made me forget my troubled day as we became fast friends. I heard plenty about the wild antics he and his partner had been part of and wanted to hear more, but the hour was getting late. I didn't have to go to work the next day, but I felt like I had a million things to do to get my life back to normal. But I also dreaded being there alone.

"Would you come back to my place, Henry?" I asked.

"Sure, what do you have in mind?"

"I think I just want some strong, manly detective to look around my place before I get into bed alone. Would you mind?"

Without a moment of hesitation, Henry replied, "Well, you don't need to get in bed alone. I could keep you company."

Maybe it was the stress talking, but even with my heart in my throat, I said, "Only if you promise to handcuff me to the bed." It was out of my mouth and spoken; impossible to retrieve.

"I have completely come unhinged!" I thought, searching his face for a response. My sensible brain was demanding that I slow down and leave this guy alone for the night, but my wild girl brain was ready, willing and able to take advantage of this fine, public servant. I couldn't deny the attraction; Henry was hard looking, but definitely in a good way. He gave me a knowing smile and called for the check. "Well, I seem to have done it again," I thought as we left.

I had a few drinks, and I heard trauma could cause adrenaline to flow fast. I thought I needed to blame this outrageous behavior on something! Whatever it was, I was horny and nearly beside myself. When we reached the apartment, Henry took the keys and walked around the place turning on lights and looking into closets. Ralph escorted him about. I felt secure and happy. He decided to play my protector for the evening.

"Are you going to get into trouble staying here with me?" I asked.

"It's OK. I'm not in any relationship right now," he confessed.

"I meant with your job."

"Well, this will be our little secret, alright?"

"Secret? Hmmm.... So, how much money do you have?" I asked, teasingly.

"Blackmailing me already? I could pay you in other ways," he said, his voice sexy and low.

He came close and pulled me into his arms. Ralph tried to nudge between us. His body was rock solid and so was Ralph's. He kissed me from my forehead down to the pulse beat on my neck. I was ready, urgently ready, and he moved ahead as fast as my gestures showed the way. I started "signaling" as fast as I could, unbuttoning his shirt as quickly as my fingers could move. We left a trail of clothing from the den straight to the bedroom. Ralph took his clue and headed for the den. Henry was so beautiful; I could hardly wait to get the next thing off him. I jumped on him as soon as we were in reach of the bed, and we tossed around kissing and fondling each other. In a pause in the action, he untangled himself and got off the bed.

"I'll be right back," he said.

"Where are you going?" I moaned.

"I have to grab something. One sec."

I could hear him going through his clothes and hurrying back to the bedroom. He paused at the door so I could take in his gorgeous body, handcuffs dangling from his fingers.

I enjoyed being in "protective custody!"

Lesson learned– When detectives come to investigate, make sure you're prepared to give the investigating officer everything he needs. You might just like being handcuffed for the night and enjoying the protective custody!

39

ALEX – KISSING SHOULD BE OUTLAWED

I was taking an evening computer class with a tall, fair-skinned and very gorgeous teacher named Alex. The class rumor-mill circulated he was divorced with one son. I could see myself going out with him, just to sample what looked to be the most kissable lips this side of the Atlantic.

A couple of weeks into the term, I hit a difficult section and couldn't figure out how to maneuver through a program. Nothing I tried made sense, and for the first time, I felt truly stuck, which left me frustrated and grouchy. I almost skipped class, but I paid a lot of money for it and didn't want to fall behind. My classmates, I'm sure, were a little surprised with my attitude that night, and some of them let me know they were concerned.

Until this particular class, I'd been cheerful, laughing and happy. That night, I felt like I really could scream and throw something. It wasn't just one thing about the program; it was a lot of little things balling up into a mountain of frustration. The first hour was a blur of one agonizing thing after another, and the worst of it came after the break when we practiced on our own. In minutes I felt lost, confused and helpless. I felt like I was on PMS overload.

Alex came up behind me and looked at my computer screen. "It isn't working," I said. "This computer is just not working at all." Alex chuckled and told me all the computers worked fine that morning. I snapped at him and sarcastically said that perhaps someone broke mine, as it certainly wasn't working now. Alex calmly reached around me and typed a few keys and poof, my screen was back on like it was supposed to be.

I felt like an idiot. The folks around me kept quiet and looked at their own work, but I was horribly embarrassed. I asked to be excused from the class, and he backed away with concern in his eyes. I don't think he realized how frustrated I'd become. I practically ran to the bathroom, and sat in a stall and cried like there was no tomorrow, sobbing until I could finally get control over myself. I decided enough was enough and went to the sink to wash my face and fix my hair. Looking in the mirror, I told myself everything was going to be alright. This too shall pass.

Class was ending when I got back, and Alex asked me to stay for a minute. He wanted to know what was going on because he missed the "old me." I didn't want to share my problems with him, but he reassured me that he was a good listener and would give me a strong shoulder to cry on if I wanted it. He took both my hands and rubbed them gently. His hands were surprisingly warm and smooth.

He had nice, strong hands and a kind, gentle face, but when I looked up I recognized a mischievous twinkle in his eyes. In spite of my rotten mood I instantly felt aroused. "What is the matter with me," I thought. "This nice man offers comfort and I see sexy." I thanked him for his concern and gathered my things, ready to leave my problems behind. Alex told me he could see the class had really gotten to me and offered to walk me to my car.

On the way, he insisted he follow me home, and I thought, "Why not? I could use a shoulder to cry on, and despite the lateness of the day, he still smelled damn good." I definitely didn't want to be alone and miserable. At my house, Alex walked me to the door and opened it. I asked him if he wanted something to drink, offering a glass of wine. He came in; I poured two drinks and we sat on the couch. I was sure he could tell that I was still upset about the class. I couldn't focus at all on any romantic potential. I couldn't bring myself to care that the owner of perhaps the most luscious lips in the West was sitting knee to knee with me, on my couch, in private. I was so stuck in my misery that it hardly occurred to me that Alex might be there for more than giving me a little comfort; he could possible give a lot. My sexy thoughts were quickly returning....

I stared at my glass while he made small talk. "Class this..." and "...sometimes computers can be that...." I wasn't following the conversation at all and responded with a meaningless grunt each time he spoke, avoiding his eyes. He finally reached over to lift my face, and I saw that same mischievous twinkle and passion-filled smile. His expression brought me back to the realization that I had the "most kissable lips" man in my living room. I managed a lusty smile.

"You need to unwind in a hot bath. You go have a good soak, and I'll see what I can put together for dinner. You'll see, and you'll feel better." I wasn't hungry, though I should have been. My despair was lingering, and I felt as though I wasn't good for anything. Alex was right and I obeyed, heading into the bathroom like a woman on a mission. I was tired of these conflicting emotions. I ran the water as hot as I could stand it and added all kinds of aromatherapy, anything I could find. The bath smelled divine as I slowly lowered myself in. It was a haven for sure.

I turned on the Jacuzzi jets and lay back, closing my eyes. Tension started to slip away at last. Each breath felt like letting go of another piece of my terrible day. I sank into the sensation until I was completely at rest; peaceful. The glass of iced bourbon was adding to the relaxation, too. I took a piece of ice and ran it across my face and chest. The contrasting sensations made me relax even more. After a while, I heard a soft knock on the door and realized that I'd totally forgotten Alex! Damn these iced bourbon, Jacuzzi baths!

Through the door, he asked if he could come in. I thought it would be fine as he wouldn't see through all the bubbles. He came in and commented on the fragrance and how good it smelled. Kneeling next to me, he asked if I wanted him to wash my back. What another delight! Instead, I handed him another piece of ice and told him to run it across my back. Please! The shivers were enchanting!

"I really give a good massage, too," he said, finding my loofah and starting on my shoulders again. He massaged and scrubbed down my back, and I could feel even more tension leaving my body. I was going to be liquefied in a minute. I didn't analyze how or why, but my worries were gone, and I felt completely comfortable with him. His touch made me think of being pampered by a masseuse in a spa, and I loved every second of it. He rubbed all the way down to my buttocks and back up to my shoulders, and then pushed me back against the tub. He rubbed down my front and then lifted up one leg and then the other, massaging firmly and smoothly. I could tell that he knew precisely what he was doing, for therapy as well as romance. He was very comfortable being my masseuse.

I grinned at him and said, "Well, now you're all wet, too." Smiling, he said, "What's a little water among friends? I can't give you a proper massage this way. Finish up your bath and come lie down for me. I'll give you one of my best, specialty massages. I promise you've never had one like it."

I didn't know if I could stand anymore massaging, and I was exhausted, but I was game to go on to the next step. I wasn't going to miss his specialty because of exhaustion. If nothing else, I wanted a taste of those juicy lips! I finished with a quick rinse in the shower, wrapped a large towel around me, and entered my now romantic, candlelit bedroom. Mmmmm, sexy lips and suave, too! He hunted around and found all kinds of candles, and was standing by the bed with only his pants on. He said it was now his turn to shower and highly suggested I lie down and relax.

As I lay there, I drifted into the fantasy of taking my crisp, clean sheets for a ride with Alex Sexy Lips. I had a fine fantasy going, too, when I heard the shower stop, and he emerged from the bathroom. Squinting, I saw his candlelit form, that is was tall, very handsome, very naked and wet. Good lord, what was an exhausted woman to do with all that sexiness? I'm sure I was going to work it out and develop all kinds of energy.

I could feel the day's heaviness trying to carry me into that slumber, but I fought like hell as I watched him come across the room. Unable to win the fight, I closed my eyes. In a moment, he was on the bed pulling back the covers. He told me to imagine what it would feel like to be kissed all over my body. I had been kissed many times before, so I didn't quite know what he meant until he began. I'm awake now, hot dammit!

He started at the very top of my head, touching and massaging with his fingers and then kissing where they had been. He gracefully traced his touches and kisses down my face and then to my throat. He circled my breast and then my stomach, kissed his way across my belly button and then my hips, around my scented pleasure and down my thighs. Without stopping, he kissed my knees, lifted my legs to touch and kiss the back of my knees (a first for me, I thought), my shins, ankles and feet. He didn't go too quickly; didn't concentrate on any one area, just carefully and thoroughly kissed every inch of skin. Fully relaxed and feeling extremely regal, all I could do was enjoy each new sensation. His "specialty massage" was perfectly paced for my limp state of mind.

He gathered each toe for a kiss and sucked a few, then turned me over. He kissed my arches and then my heels and made his way up my calves and to the back of my knees again. I was being lovingly and amazingly "tortured" and it was the most tremendous sensation. I couldn't help but smile and groan and moan. I couldn't have fallen asleep again, if I tried.

I had to bite my lip as he continued his journey up my thighs and then onto my rump. He kissed his way onto my lower back, then delicately licked and kissed each vertebrae up my spine, around my shoulders and then to the back of my neck. He stretched up to kiss my ears and whispered softly that he was going to kiss me again, this time only on one part of my body. I was putty in his hands and a goner, with my eyes closed but far from asleep.

He turned me over, spread my legs and kissed me deliberately in my scented wet center. He kissed and licked, building his intensity only slightly. He just kept going, a little more and a lot more, until I shuddered quietly, clenched and relaxed straight into the slumber that had been pulling at me. As I fell asleep, the last thing I felt was him pulling the covers back over me.

When I next saw Alex in class, I thanked him for helping to sooth away my despair with such enjoyable kisses. My classmate overheard me and whispered, "Did you kiss Alex??" Smiling, I said, "Well, no, actually he kissed me." She tried to get me to spill the beans, but I told her that was all I was going to say. Wink, wink!

Lesson learned– Kissing is an art form, so powerful in the hands of a master, that perhaps it should be outlawed in many states. I would, however, gladly live in any of them as long as I got to participate in the crimes! We also never kiss and tell any part of the story!

40

STEPHAN – THE ISLAND PLEASER

As the first days of summer offered a chance to escape, two of my friends, my sister and I took a cruise to the Caribbean. The four of us agreed to single cabins on the same deck to stay close, but to have our privacy. I loved my older sister, but wondered if she would try to curtail my adventurous nature. She was a single beauty and attracted men all the time, but she was much more reserved and didn't let her hair down the way I liked to. So I thought!

The first morning out we all met at the breakfast buffet. I was a little sick that morning, still trying to get used to the sounds and motion of the ocean, and the surprisingly tiny cabin. Cramped little spaces and my voluptuous figure are a mismatch at the best of times, so I hated the tiny bed and had even more trouble in the tiny bathroom. I could barely sit on the toilet, and I could brush my teeth and turn on the shower if I held my elbows out at my sides.

It was at least 10:30 a.m. by the time I managed to meet everyone in the cavernous and mostly empty dining room. I found my friends and sister in a corner laughing and drinking coffee. The place smelled divine with all the buffets, and I started feeling a little better the moment I got within smelling range of the food.

The minute they saw me, my entourage stood and started singing to me. I should have expected a fun start to the day and smiled in anticipation of a very happy, fun-filled birthday. Part of my motive for going on the trip was to celebrate my 35th birthday, and my "posse" was letting me know they were going to see to it that I had a grand time.

Breakfast was just the start as they laid out their plans for the day, with all sorts of entertainment lined up, ending with an on-board comedy show. I was "Birthday Girl and Queen for a Day" as they put a tiara on my head and served me breakfast. People passing by wished me a very happy birthday also, and I felt totally special. All of a sudden, a crew member pulled my sister aside for something, but I was occupied, happily munching away, while the girls walked me through their plans for the rest of the day.

When the ship docked in Puerto Rico, shortly after I finished breakfast, we headed to the balconies to watch as we came into port. My sister rejoined us at the railing, grinning like a Cheshire cat. I knew that sweet thing must have done something good to put that grin on her face. I couldn't help but wonder what it might be. I was sure her plans for my day had a secret surprise and maybe more than one. I could only be certain she was up to something, and my first clue was that my sister and the girls had scheduled a tour of the rum factory. This is either going to be very, very good, or very, very bad, I thought, or perhaps a bit of both!

We toured the factory, sampling every variety of rum within reach. A lubricated tourist is a happy tourist! I valiantly sampled until I was about half cross-eyed. I found a favorite, a coconut flavored rum. It would make great piña colodas, I imagined, as I sampled it a few more times, just to be sure. I purchased three bottles. The trip was off to a great start as far as I was concerned!

We had a nice variety of flavors, and I noted that my sister had found a potent bottle of 150 proof. She was apparently getting in the spirit of things and planned on a very fun-filled cruise! Unfortunately, we found out you have to hand in your alcohol until the ship returns to home port. We grumbled a lot and laughingly agreed that it meant somebody was going to be getting blitzed when we got home. We

Josaphine's Lessons

amended our plans on the fly so that, meanwhile, we'd get more use out of the on-board bars....Oh damn! We all had a nice little buzz by the time we returned to our cabins to rest and get ready for dinner. Then, we would head to the comedy show.

My nap was interrupted by a soft knock at the door. I sleepily looked out the peephole to see my sister and someone else. Fitting three people into the cabin was a chore, but we squeezed in, and I sat on the end of the bed rubbing my eyes clear to ogle the good looking couple. My sister had snagged a seriously handsome hunk and my, oh my, he was pleasing to look at. I hungrily took in his tight, sexy shirt and his handsome, strong-jawed face as my sister made the introductions.

His name was Stephan, and he was a native of the islands. He smiled and took my hand in his and caressed it. I felt excited as goose pimples raced up my arm, all the way to my nipples from his touch. His caress redefined "Latin lover" in about five seconds flat. My sister went on to say that since it was my birthday, Stephan was my escort for the evening. The girls had chipped in and he was my birthday present! Yummy!

My mouth fell open in complete disbelief. My eyes must have been the size of plates as my sister put her hand under my chin and told me to stop drooling. I was so stunned, it was all I could do to laugh and try to gain control of my face!

Stephan sparkled a pearly white smile at me, and I just sat there, speechless. He told me in his wonderful accent how lovely I was, and that he couldn't wait to pick me up at a quarter past seven for our dinner reservation. He advised me to dress nicely for the evening and restaurant, saying it would be "very elegant indeed." He stood, still holding my hand, kissing my hand, while caressing my wrist, finishing his exit with another award-winning smile.

The moment the door closed, I nearly screamed at my sister, "What the hell? How did, and where did you get that tall drink of mocha chocolate latte from?" She cracked up laughing and enjoying every moment of my reaction. The more incoherent and flabbergasted I was, the harder she laughed. If there had been enough room,

I'm sure she would have rolled around in stitches. Smacking myself mentally, I put two and two together, remembering her rendezvous with the crew member at breakfast.

Finally, she recovered enough to tell me the deal: Stephan would do anything I wanted for the evening. Everything had been prearranged and paid for and they'd see me at dinner. She hugged and kissed me, and told me to have a fantastic time. She left the cabin and I fell back onto the bed wondering what I was going to wear. And does "anything I want" really mean "anything?"

Stephan picked me up exactly on time, dressed in a dark grey, pin-striped, Armani suit with a gorgeous, mauve, striped tie and escorted me upstairs. That man oozed sexuality all the way from his suave, black shiny hair, down to his Johnston & Murphy's. He matched perfectly to my backless, dark grey, silky soft, cocktail dress, with matching, mauve Stilettos.

We walked down the hall to the elevators and rode it up and up and up until it hit the top deck, and we exited at the entrance to a very exclusive-looking restaurant. Stephan told me it was the private dining quarters of the who's who list. I smiled nervously and thought I was way out of my league, but I was determined to suck it in and enjoy every moment. We were the last to be seated at a table for eight, with my sister and friends filling the table, each of them with their own date. The waiter poured my champagne and whispered happy birthday. I blushed, wondering who *didn't* know it was my special day.

I couldn't imagine where they'd found these beautiful Island men, but they looked very much the Island pleasers. Stephan stood up and toasted my birthday and the festivities began. We ate, drank, and laughed for hours and then drank some more. In those posh surroundings we weren't rushed at all, and we squeezed every ounce of fun out of our time. We finally left dinner and headed to the comedy club a little early, planning plenty of time to get a good seat. We were all happy, full and pleasantly tipsy.

Stephan held me close as we walked along the deck, a perfect gentleman. I was happy I had removed my Stilettos. The wind was

Josaphine's Lessons

fresh and wild, and I felt the salt licking my face as it blew up from the ocean. The atmosphere was perfect, and we strolled along as if we had all night to gaze at the moon and the stars. It was so picture perfect that I wished time would pause just a moment.

I reflected on the story-book perfection my birthday was turning out to be, and how thankful I was to have such great friends and my sister to share it with. Stephan stopped at the railing and bracketed me with his hands. I shivered, not from the chill of the ocean, though. He leaned, into me and I inhaled as much air as I could, trying to drink in every moment. He quietly said, "I wonder, do you taste as fine as you look?" With anyone else and at any other time, that line would have been out-of-bounds corny, but coming from his lips as he gently kissed me, it was like a spoken caress. He kissed softly along my neck, but I could tell he wanted more. His pants didn't hide his excited member. The rest of the group had gone ahead, but Stephan kept me pinned there. As he expertly nuzzled closer, he asked me in a whisper if I really wanted to see the show.

I heard myself say, "If the choice is time with you or a show, then no, the show can be history." He took my hands and led me to another part of the ship where there was an enclosed pool and Jacuzzi. He opened the doors and led me to the warm, bubbling water. I thought the pool should have been closed, but he seemed so deft and to know what he was doing, that I wasn't going to question anything. He helped me undress to my undergarments and guided me slowly into the hot tub. He followed soon after, clad only in tight fitting boxers. They hugged him closely and I stared unabashed, thinking I'd love to be that close to him. I wasn't going to have to wait long.

He sat next to me and asked what I wanted for my birthday. Good Heavens, another clichéd line, and Praise the Lord, it was working like a charm. I got flustered, glancing away, trying to think how to say what I really wanted. "But hell," I reminded myself, "I'm already half naked and this handsome Island hunk is, after all, supposed to be mine for the night." He began massaging my shoulders and I sank down, relaxing into his hands. The water and the heat felt so good. I drifted and nearly forgot where I was. "You," I said in a voice I didn't quite recognize, "I want you for my birthday."

He smiled, and I knew he expected my request. Without hesitation, he stood and took off his briefs. He was hard as a rock, though I hadn't touched him at all. He then took off my bra and panties and put on a condom. I found myself wondering momentarily where it had been hidden, and how he had sprung to readiness so easily, but I really didn't care. He was an artist, every move perfect, sucking first one boob and then the other as he caressed me with his hands. He was strong, masculine, completely in control. I stood and he turned me around, bending me over the tub. He entered me from behind, slowly, thick and hard. I gasped for air as he moved in and out to his own time. He stopped after a few strong strokes and turned me back around, helping me out of the tub. He kissed me so hard I lost my balance, but he held me up effortlessly. He backed me up to a chaise lounge and followed me down onto it. He put my legs around his waist and plunged in with a fury. I came with a scream that must have sounded like a blast from the ship's horn. He covered my cry with a kiss until I quieted, then muttered incomprehensible words as his own release left him shuddering against me. He collapsed on top of me holding on as though we were welded together. Finally, he lifted up and asked to take me back to my cabin. I was weak-kneed and had no idea how I was supposed to walk. He brought my dress, bra and panties to me and then put on his clothes. The reality that my undergarments were wet was far from my mind.

As he escorted me to my cabin, his accent seemed more defined—even sexier than before. When we reached my door, I was ready to say good night but he came inside, set me on the tiny bed and called for room service to bring champagne. He quickly reassured me that the night was too young and the love too good to part so soon.

He wanted me naked and he wanted it without delay. He said, "For this birthday, I intend to please you until you cannot walk for the rest of your trip." I was ecstatic over and over that he came fully dressed for the after-party.

"Oh, my, my, my! I'm ready for you to go for it!" was all I could say as he began to kiss my clothes off me. He was confident, even in that cramped little space, sliding my things off with a fine expertise. He was as smooth and ready for love the second time as he had been the first, only this time lasted longer and was, if anything, better. Consummate professional that he was, Stephan made the second orgasm all about me and my pleasure. The champagne arrived with perfect timing not long after we scaled to the heavens, and we toasted one last time to my fabulous 35th year.

Lesson learned– If you happen to get an Island pleaser as a present, relax and enjoy. Don't forget to thank your friends! While the hot-blooded Island lover is with you, your pleasure is his entire reason for living. Just smile, enjoy your adventure, and say, "Happy Birthday Me!"

ABOUT THE AUTHOR

As a retired Special Education teacher, widow and mother of a teenager, G.A. Harvey grew up in the New England area, the youngest of eight children. When she was in the third grade, she discovered that she could tell stories about her family and friends, keeping everyone's attention.

Harvey began developing her writing skills in the early 1980s. During this time, she participated in, and taught several writing classes for students for many years.

Often, she encountered many conversations on sexual activities with her peers, as well as others', and developed Josaphine from them.

Now, Josaphine has her own stories to tell that are right interesting, and some sexual trysts will be worth repeating to your friends. Or, just make you say "damn!"

G.A. Harvey and her daughter live in the Atlanta, Georgia, area.